Talefade

Gillian Shimwell

Talefade

Written by

Gillian Shimwell

First Published in 2025 by Fantastic Books Publishing
Cover design by Ramon Marett

ISBN (ebook): 978-1-914060-62-5
ISBN (paperback): 978-1-914060-63-2

Copyright © Gillian Shimwell

The right of Gillian Shimwell to be identified as the author of this book has been asserted by her in accordance with the Copyright, Designs and Patents Act 1998.

All rights reserved.

All rights reserved. No part of this publication may be reproduced, stored in or introduced into a retrieval system or transmitted, in any form, or by any means (electronic, mechanical, photocopying, recording or otherwise) without the prior written permission of the publisher or unless such copying is done under a current Copyright Licensing Agency license. Any person who does any unauthorised act in relation to this publication may be liable to criminal prosecution and civil claims for damages.

Acknowledgements

I would like to thank folklorist Mark Henderson for his friendship and invaluable critical support, encouragement and technical help.

My friend Helen Moat, travel writer and friend, for her honest appraisals.

Suzanne Elvidge, for advising me on what to leave out.

Fantastic Books Publishing, for the opportunity and the challenge.

Matlock Storytelling Café, for the tales I learned and the space to tell.

Prologue: Falling Tales

'You're getting very thin,' said one to the other. 'I can see right through you.'

'Ha. We've always been able to see through you –' a sideways, rustling remark, ending in a cough.

They – the Tales, the themes and stories of our world – were lying amongst the cobwebs in the Bookless Library. They could barely see each other because they were losing heart, though they would always hear each other's voices. Only when they spoke would they know themselves to be surviving still, but only when told again by mortals would they thrive and gain eternal vigour.

'Fat chance of that happening,' creaked the Saga. None had said a word on the subject; it was, simply, always on their minds.

A bird flew in through the open window, a strange and crazy bird incompetent at flight, or perhaps a giant moth … No, it was a page, a crumpled piece of paper, with words all over its face and backside.

'Spy,' whispered invisibly around the room. 'Infiltrator.'

The page unpeeled itself from the floor and straightened up as much as it could.

'Gentlemen,' it began, 'unless we work together we are all doomed.'

'We know what you're up to. Work together, co-operate, then bam – we'll all be trapped, stiffs made of ink with no power to change. No reader can change a Tale like a living listener, the flame reflected in his eyes and the cold at his back –'

'You mistake me! I – all of my kind – we preserve, we don't imprison. Besides, we are in danger, too. Put it this way: no one ever burned a spoken word.' A sly look crept across the printed face. 'Also, once printed, we can't betray ourselves. Only by interference and rewriting, or a bad adaptation, can our true meaning be sullied.'

An uncomfortable thought shifted the cobwebs on the shelves. The page realised that some of the Tales had briefly faded into visibility and out again. He had struck a nerve.

As if in answer to a prompt there was a flurry of disordered light, like satin, a stench of sweat and powder. A lone balloon rose, then vanished in the rafters. Something overpowering dropped itself all over the room. As it did so, there was a loud "pop".

'That's the other one gone,' in a coarse, deep voice.

There was a frozen pause.

'Oh, I know you're all 'ere, the lot of you. Oh yes you are. You made your feelings known when I took my chance, and nowt's changed except my wigs. Well, listen, boys and girls, I'm as valid an art form as any of you, and I'm visible. Look behind you! Aye, I know you've turned your backs. I tried at the time, but you wouldn't be told, none of you. And now … well, you're not being told, are you? What's this, stuck to my foot?'

'It's me,' mumbled the page. 'Please be very careful.'

'Oh, we're always very careful. We don't want a mess, do we? Sorry about that …' as the page was peeled off and held up, limp and gasping, for inspection. 'Just a bit of wet on my shoe from the slosh. I'll warm you up in my corset. Plenty of room now the balloons are gone. Now, what's all this about?'

All began to speak, or hiss, until –

'Please.'

A soft but clear voice; kind, yet firm. There was a movement, and the Tale whose voice had melted their discord faded into view; a slender, pale mauve shape moving with cautious grace seated herself between Ellafella and the others.

'I'd like everyone to hear me. If we tell ourselves, we will know. I'm sorry, I'm quite … Simple. I know what I mean to say …'

'Don't you put yourself down, pet. There's as much in you as in any of these longwinded arm wavers.'

'Thank you. Everyone – I want everyone to hear.'

'Ooh, I was forgetting this little rascal.'

Ellafella fished the crumpled page from his gown and spread it out on his lap.

'That's an outsider!' A voice stung the air.

'Whisht, you. Let her speak.'

The Farmer's Three Children

There was a farmer.

He had three children grown to adulthood. He wanted to … Yes, he was still strong, but …

He remembered his own father and grandfather, dead at the plough, working to the second their souls flew. He decided to give the farm to one of his grown family and take some ease before he died; perhaps travel to the sea, which he had never seen, and spend more time with his friend the Squire.

One evening, as he sat opposite the Squire up at the Hall, sharing a glass and a pipe by the fire, he spoke out.

'I want to give over the farm. Have a little ease before I die.'

'Good notion, my friend.'

'Aye, but it's not so simple. Made the decision all right but – how to go about it? No, no, I'll not just hand it to the elder boy. You know him. And the second …?'

'You're not sure he's up to it? Because your eldest … he doesn't get his hands dirty, I grant you that. Surely he might rise to the challenge? You don't know his mettle.'

The Squire gazed into the flames and the men sat the way friends can – and ofttimes strangers too, in Northern Dales – in wordless trust and mutuality.

'Hah!' the Squire barked. 'Listen, friend, though you're their father, you don't know all about them. You need to try them. Listen to me …'

The next morning at breakfast, as they drained their small

beer and the daughter cleared the platters, the farmer bade his sons wait, for he had something to say. He announced his intention to hand over the farm to the son who could fill the house with something most precious. It must be filled entirely, with no space for a draught to blow through, no crack for light to shine.

All day, as the eldest worked at the accounts, he wondered what was most precious, what would prove his fitness to take the farm. That same evening, preparing to visit his sweetheart in the town, his own reflection told him: as he gazed into the brown-mottled glass, the single candle in the room glinted on the plain gold pin he fastened. What could be better than gold? Plenty of gold would keep the farm going; choosing it would prove him ambitious; and he was certain that he could fill the house.

He spent the next day gathering all the gold he could, issuing receipts to friends and tradesmen, whilst the rest of the family heaved the furniture on to carts and took it to store in the Squire's spare rooms.

When the farmer drove up to his house the following noon, he blinked at the sight. The windows blazed with gold, reflecting the fury of the sun's power. The old man pressed against the door, which was as firm as a cliff. He climbed the ladder to the upper floor.

Somewhere deep in the old farmer's heart quivered an anxiety that his elder son might win, but he had not the words to explain what it could mean. When he looked through the window he could see the rafters; and a gleam of light from the opposite window, shining across the sunken pile of gold.

The elder boy would not receive the farm.

When all the gold had been returned and the daughter had

swept even the gold dust from the corners and put it into little twists of paper, the second son could take his turn. He was generally considered to be more given to the toil of the farm than his brother because he loved the open air, and he was broad-built and reserved in manner.

He decided that the thing most precious to him was sweet rest and comfort at the day's end. He gathered all the feathers he could find, even robbing the nests of birds, even splitting the quilts his mother had made for each of them, beginning with the faded one that had lain on the bed in which his father now slept alone.

When the father came to see the house next morning, the windowpanes were pressed to breaking with the weight of feathers. When he climbed up to peer into the windows, there was no light or sight of surfaces; all was crammed.

The farmer bit his bottom lip and climbed on to the roof, sitting aside to peer – yes, down into the chimney, into the stack below, where he could see the sooty surface of the feather pile; a few downy fragments whirled free, and away they danced.

The second boy would not receive the farm.

The farmer was honour-bound to test his daughter, too. He wondered who might be fit to manage the farm or perhaps be a useful husband. Nevertheless, she must take her turn.

The daughter knew it was her turn the next day. She abandoned her task – she was in the Squire's boot-room, stuffing the quilts and pinning the feathers into little pockets ready to sew – to prepare for her try.

Honestly, she was unsure whether she wanted to own the whole farm. She thought it might be best to take her harp on her back, to sit and practise whilst she considered what to do.

So just after breakfast she set off and walked up to her home and sat in the settle by the bare stone hearth, which, being affixed to the panelling, had not been taken to the Hall.

Eventually, playing all the tunes her teacher had taught her, and a few plucked from her own dreams, she forgot the inheritance and played the becks and hills, the hawthorn and the tumbling stones, the secret dens, and the first harebells peeping. She played the cry of the cade lamb, the smell of new bread, and the whip and flap of line-hung sheets.

The farmer drew up outside his home. He put his shoulder to the door and nearly fell on to the flags. Steadying himself, he held his breath as a trickling melody reached his ear. He went into the parlour, where he thought his daughter might have set out food or blankets; there was nothing but that fairy sound. He peeped into the kitchen, and there she was, swaying, her back toward him.

Withdrawing, he climbed the stairs with the lilting at his heels, and into every chamber. Even when he climbed and sat astride the roof, the music danced up to meet him.

That is how the daughter inherited the farm.

The Quest

After three days of argument, it was agreed that the Tales should venture into the world to observe and assess the state of things. They would not seek to communicate with mortals, but simply watch the behaviour of these strange, mutant creatures for a time; then, when they returned home to the bookless library, they would either make a plan – or abandon themselves, and humankind, to oblivion.

On the first day of their Quest, the Tales awoke on a misty fen, a distant moan echoing around them.

OKIKU: We are all Ghosts, Waiting to be Born

Words are too heavy, like masonry.
    We are all ghosts, waiting to be born.
    The season can be described. Can it be conjured?
    My uncle lives in a castle.
    Too grand.
    The castle is a small one, mostly a museum now, and my uncle – whose wife had connections to the defunct family – had rooms in the part overlooking the city. He looks after the museum.
    My parents, when I told them I wanted to be independent and not marry, had agreed to let me go to the city. I had studied at the Kunitachi College, and had not been guided into teaching but encouraged to consider a professional career. My parents' notion of allowing me to follow my vision was to secure me a teaching post at a small private centre owned by a friend of theirs, and to persuade my uncle to give me a home. If, they said, I had the dedication to practise, and if I would get myself some opportunities, playing with a cultural group or convincing some local business to fund a concert, perhaps if I won a national competition, then I would indeed deserve success. No attainment was worth anything without sacrifice.
    My life with my uncle, as I anticipated it in the first days, would reflect my parents' values admirably. The centre employed me on three days of the week to do music and any

other duties as required. My uncle required me to look after the flat, shop for food, prepare meals. When he was not out at night, he sat and watched television, so practice was impossible.

On the first free day, my uncle showed me how to clean the flat. His steady thoroughness, his complete absorption in each task, made me squirm inwardly, like a child. He stood by my elbow on the second day, watching me try to replicate his method. Once, he let me fold all the fine cotton cloths in the way my mother had taught me – perfectly neatly, as I thought. Just as I was putting them away, he stopped me and shook them all out and demonstrated his preferred method with one; then, with a little 'hm' in his throat, he went into his room.

Even after three weeks I felt he was a stranger.

The flat was sparsely furnished, with furniture that could have come from an office. It took only a couple of hours to clean quite thoroughly, but uncle always found something else to occupy my time.

At supper one night he unfolded a packet of stiff paper, nudged it across the table and nodded an invitation to try the confection, a pale green moist cake. I took an inch square, and he told me:

'Another. Take your time. Yes? I want you to find the recipe. I bought this, but your aunt could make better. I'd like the fragrance in my house again.'

After delivering this almost poetic sliver of himself, he stood, tucked the newspaper under his arm and sat, half watching a concert of sentimental pop music on the TV, half reading the paper, filling the room with cigarette smoke – against which I clamped my throat, resenting the effect on my voice, if I ever got to sing to my own accompaniment again.

The following day he went out in the afternoon. He left me on the corridor outside the flat to search the contents of a great chest, where my aunt's things were stored. He watched as I opened up the complex puzzle of the chest, dropping his keys and rolled-up cotton cap on to the top of the chest to help me remove one of the heavier drawers. He was already wearing his denim cap, and I wondered why he had another. Perhaps he and his old friends all wore one on their trips to the country. I wondered whether my aunt had ever met his friends.

The aunt I had never known seemed to grow out of the chest, surrounding me as I emptied each compartment; though a papery sweetness, a faded stillness, underlined her absence. My living grandmother has older clothes, her rooms unchanged in fifty years, but there is none of the listening, melancholy quality that dwells among the trappings of the dead.

Most of the objects I found were so conventional that they concealed my aunt's uniqueness. Little dolls, fans, traditional gifts or souvenirs – the light-headed sense of encounter that I had experienced at first, unfolding a broad sash, home-made and embroidered, flattened into disconnected irritation. This delving would lead to nothing but wasted time; I could be practising. I would not find the woman my uncle had married, and it didn't matter. I just needed to find the recipe.

It jolted me, then, to find a photograph of a young man in a broken frame. If alive, he would now be in his sixties. It was a formal portrait; he was handsome. I gazed into the eyes and was shocked by a flash of – insight? Imagination? The sense that the broken frame had been flung and stamped on and the pieces hastily thrust into the parcel. Who was the young man? Why, when he put my aunt's things away, had my uncle not got rid of the frame?

Again, I shook myself and tried to hurry my efforts. Perhaps my parents had been right to test my dedication. I was too easily distracted.

The gloomy height of the wooden roof, the open space of the silent staircase and the breadth of the corridor began to oppress me with a sensation of falling, or of being fallen on, by the weight of all the space inside the castle. It was an uneasy antithesis of the expansive joy felt on a mountain top with an ocean view.

The last box I opened contained tea plates of porcelain; smoothly pure white, with a shallow curve, the underside painted with a bone green moon, a drift of willow across its face and a blush of cloud above. I put the plates on the chest, meaning to take them into the flat and make a cake from my grandmother's recipe to compensate my uncle for my failure.

There were no keys on the chest.

Recalling my uncle's distracted air and the two denim caps, I realised that he had taken the spare key along with everything he'd swept into his pockets to hurry off, locking the flat from the inside and going out the back way. Why had he even needed to lock the flat, as I was only just outside?

There was a draught blowing under the door, so a window was open somewhere. I would need to go out through the museum, into the garden and up the wooden steps. Not wanting to leave the plates, I cushioned them with old fabric and put them into a misshapen straw beach bag from the chest.

I had to negotiate a labyrinth of corridors and rooms beyond rooms, all unknown and confusing. Once, I turned a corner and was startled by a group of people in a painted room, so still they seemed as startled as I was, as still as cats about to pounce. The corridor creaked, its floor singing at my back as I sped along. I turned another corner and was shaken to see the same stiff arrangement, their backs to me.

I went down another shadowy staircase, expecting soon to be out. There was a garden door that I could open, and, as long as I remembered to tell my uncle so he could check it on his rounds, there would be no risk. I saw the door and made for it, clutching the straw bag like a baby. The door was unlocked. It swung open on to an inner courtyard.

There was nowhere to sit, no doors leading to other parts of the castle. At least I had the sky above me. I considered what to do. I could go back inside and try to find a better route back to the flat, or into the garden. When my uncle had taken me through on my arrival, it had been nowhere near as confusing. Looking up at the looming walls and the windows, I decided not to re-enter.

What if my uncle never returned? If he was invited to stay out with his friends, or had been in an accident? I imagined the telephone ringing in the flat. Was the castle open to visitors this week?

There was a well in the middle of the courtyard. I looked into it; there was no sign of water.

Eventually, I decided I should do something. I began to walk around the edges of the courtyard. Behind a small tree, where the wall seemed continuous, there was a kind of fold or pleat in the architecture. Tucked into the space between wall-ends was the turnstile from the upper terrace. I clambered and swung my legs, scooted across and stood in the garden at last.

I was cheered by the sounds of traffic on the city road.

Visitors seeking the mystery and peace of an ancient place probably regretted hearing it, but I welcomed the sweet air of mundanity after my eerie afternoon. I followed the path around to the terraces, climbing between plum trees to the foot of the wooden steps.

They were a steep climb, but I was used to carrying my instrument case up most evenings, when the door would stand open and my uncle would sometimes sit on the platform, gazing over the slope toward the distant mountains.

I looked for the open window. Although large enough to let me in, it was beyond the end of the platform, a dizzying sweep of wall above the tumbling terraces. The thought of trying to reach it made the whole world pitch and spin, and I sat on the floor for a few moments. At last, I stood and faced the evening sky, watching as it blushed to rose from blue as the waking moon appeared, a drift of grey-washed cloud burned silver, and the air began to cool.

It was dark when the door opened, slicing the platform into squares of light and shadow. My uncle left the door open, but had gone into his bathroom before I was inside. The four plates and the straw bag were on the low table. I bit my lip; I had left the bag on the well top. I sat and waited, feeling foolish and guilty.

My uncle came in, wearing a cotton robe and soft trousers, sat opposite me and waited. I began a flustered apology, but he held up his hand and tapped a forefinger on the tabletop.

'Where is the fifth plate?'

'I don't – weren't there only four?'

He gazed at me.

'If I hadn't had a lift to the front door, I'd have come up the steps, like you. The bag would have been there all night. What do you think?'

'I – I think I would have remembered.'

'Would you? I see.' He sat back. 'And you would have gone through the castle tonight to fetch it?'

'I'd have done your rounds with you – to help – and fetched them then.'

He stood up.

'Oh, no point in us both going.'

He held out the keys.

'But– the plates are here.'

'With one missing. How do I know what else you might have forgotten?'

He handed me a torch. It was small, casting less light than shadow, and the shadows leapt. My every movement was wrenched from me, as though I were a statue newly animated. As I passed the group of dummy courtiers the lights came on, and they were suddenly vivid in all their colours. The black glass eyes gleamed ironically. I found the door and ran out into the courtyard.

There was no plate on the well.

I looked down into the waterless dark, and gasped. The moon was perfectly reflected in the well.

I must be dreaming.

Somehow, my unease melted and I became curious, wondering whether the water rose and fell by some mechanism, or naturally. Perhaps its depth was illusory. I found a pebble and dropped it on to the reflected moon, which shivered into fragments with a sharp crack that made me jump.

'What are you doing?' It was my uncle. 'Hurry up, the light's on a timer.'

I followed before the door closed behind him, and turned toward the corridor.

'Where are you off to? This way.'

He stood in a doorway I hadn't seen before. We went up a few flights of featureless and well-lit stairs in less than half the time it had taken me to creep through the corridors. In the flat, the plates had been neatly stacked.

'Here. I put this in your room before you came. You should have read it. It's the visitor guide, and a plan – look, here, this is where we came in. You'll read it tonight, memorize the route. Tomorrow, after supper, I want you to find the other plate and return all five to the chest.'

From behind his newspaper, he said, 'If you broke it, tell me.'

'I would have said. No, I didn't. I put them in the bag, and that's all.'

'Good. All you have to do is find it. There's something light for your supper in the fridge. Bring me a beer. I expect you're tired.'

This was dismissal, though it was not yet ten o'clock.

There being no chair in my room, I arranged my bed so that I could read the booklet. The white paper lampshade softened the room, and, despite the hard pillow and my having to bolster myself with a rolled-up coat behind it, I managed to get comfortable.

The castle's history and architecture were easy to follow, and I saw from the plan exactly where I had gone wrong in my wanderings. There was a section of folklore in the booklet, and a whole chapter at the back with more recent history and photographs. I could find nothing to link the fairy tales to the castle and decided that they were included for a bit of romantic colour. I glanced at them. They were written in the same plain style as the information, which disappointed me.

'You don't draw me in,' I muttered. 'There's no music in your telling.'

My father, who could be distant in many ways, had once said that all art should be like music; even a few simple words on the page should change the feeling in the room. Music is a garden, a painting is a poem. Even those words were spoken with a pragmatic air, and sure enough, the next thing he said had been to tell me to help my mother clean the house.

There was a photograph in the back of the booklet. It showed a large group gathered outside the restored gatehouse some forty years ago. There were no names, just a brief note that family members, staff and the team of archaeologists had gathered for a luncheon and lecture, and to open the gatehouse with its new exhibition. I gazed at the faces until my shoulder ached; I was holding myself as stiff as the costumed figures in the castle. I lay back, easing my shoulder, but held the booklet above me, reflecting the white light, and gazed at the dull grey picture.

I was in darkness. Someone had been in the room, but when I turned on the light I was alone. The booklet lay folded on the shelf by my bed. Clearly, my uncle had seen the light under the door and found me asleep. I went to the window to open it and slid back into bed.

The next day's teaching was unmemorable except that I felt my pupils were watchful, in collusion, and somehow dulled. I had no memory of the journey home.

Perhaps I was going to be ill. When I went into the flat it was empty; the unseen radio played old pop songs and a scent of cooking hung about the place. I went into the corridor and found that the chest was open, all its compartments arranged along the floor. On top of one deep drawer lay the photograph of the young man in a new unbroken frame.

I knelt and felt along the back of the chest. What had appeared to be the solid construction had an irregular corner piece, which, I somehow knew, would open if I slid it downwards. As I did this, I heard a sound from further away; only doors and voices, which I took to be my uncle, perhaps with some private visitor; so I slid the secret door back in place and went toward the stairs.

The door was locked, so I had to take the long route through the castle. It was longer than the day before, and I saw no dressed figures in any room. I must have come upon a different route.

There was an exhibition gallery, which I entered. The permanent exhibition was of ancient pottery, and some pieces typical of the region through four hundred years, but there was a small room dedicated to contemporary work. I had none of the dread of the previous day, or the displaced nervous state of the working day just gone. Instead, I felt I was a privileged guest, suddenly enraptured by the treasures in the room and blissfully contented.

In the room of older pots there was a small tea plate of pure white porcelain. I reached into the case and delicately turned it over. There was the moon and the willow, and the grey rose tinted cloud, more perfect than I had remembered. I turned it back. Had my uncle been teasing me?

In the contemporary room I found a similar plate, unsigned and slightly less exquisite. The painting on the underside was wonderfully shaded, and I felt that someone hid behind the drooping willow branches. Next to this reproduction there was an angular plate, with elements of the design in ghostly grey on several of its facets. My parents had a flower vase in this style; a wedding present, they said. If I held the plate at any point that showed one part of the design, the others were invisible or distorted.

There was an information leaflet, which I read. On the back, a photograph of the ceramicist in his studio. As I looked, it seemed that the face could resemble either my uncle or the man in the broken frame. It kept changing. Dizzy, and less euphoric now, I made for the door.

I stood again in the courtyard, by the well.

Perhaps my uncle had family visitors; from somewhere inside I could hear children's voices counting, and squeals of laughter. Perhaps a hiding game. Yes, that was it; but I was concerned after a few minutes of counting and laughter that the game was getting too rough, the scream at the end too real.

It struck me as odd that I should be able to hear voices from inside; and at that moment the sky grew dark, and I gazed again into the well with the moon on its lacquer-smooth surface. I picked up a stone and cast it in; there was a crack, and pieces of porcelain bobbed to the surface.

'What are you playing at? You'll have to climb in and get them.' It was my uncle, in his best suit. He sounded exasperated rather than threatening, but he held the well cover in his arms. 'Look here,' he said, 'I gave you a simple job to do and you couldn't stick to it. Your eyes shouldn't see what's not for them. Don't you know that? Where's your self discipline?'

I was standing on the well. As I fell back, I shrieked, but slowly:

'Uncle, where's the child?'

I sat up in bed, feeling sick, wondering whether I had actually shouted. I waited. Nobody came.

I switched on the lamp and crept out of the room, around the flat. My uncle's snores from behind his door should have cheered me, but what if he had sent himself into my dream, leaving his snores to fool me? The furniture in the plain room seemed to be waiting. Its ordinariness was a disguise. I stared at the door that led out of the flat.

At what point had my life become the dream? If I had any sense, I would go into the corridor and – no. If I had any sense I'd go back to bed.

I had a drink of water and went to my room. The booklet was on the floor. My uncle had not come in and tidied it up, though he must have turned off the lamp. Why had I dreamt that he had folded it up, placed it neatly on the shelf?

Clearly, my anxieties about the plates, frustration with teaching, the creepy experiences of the day before, had given me nightmares. The photograph in its new reproduction frame, the folded booklet, signified my desire for answers, for order. There was nothing more to it.

The following day's teaching passed with no unusual difficulty, and the pupils behaved well, although I suspected their shy watchfulness; the dream leaked into every moment of the day, staining ordinary incidents with unnerving possibility.

I worried, too, about the fifth porcelain plate. I was certain there had been four all along. So what was my uncle playing at? He'd asked me the same question – no, that was in the dream – but there had been a dry bafflement in his tone several times since I arrived, which made me feel like a child.

Why had I dreamt that the photograph was mended? Had he forgiven his wife at last?

On the way home the bus was delayed near a ceramics gallery, and as we drew slowly alongside its sleek windows I decided to go in. I got off as soon as I could and walked back. There was nothing quite right in the gallery, but there was a bookshop. I had the same sense of joy and elegant calm that I'd experienced in the dream gallery. It may be that such places are unrelated to the shabbiness and bustle of life as it is lived; they exude such a sense of order and spacious creativity. I had no name for the potter, who in my dream had flickered in his identity like sunlight through a fence. Well, then, I could start with my uncle.

Oh, he was never a potter, said the gallery lady, but he was well known and liked. So, he was my uncle? Oh yes, he had been in management at the superior department store and sat on several charity boards. Been something of an athlete in his youth. Never an artist himself, though he had studied art history before settling to regular work and marrying my aunt. So, I was his niece? How did I like the castle?

I asked whether there had ever been exhibitions at the castle – art exhibitions, especially as my uncle had enjoyed an academic or amateur interest. Of course, I had only dreamt the exhibition that I'd visited, but it remained vivid in my mind. The lady didn't know. Despite her apparent familiarity with my uncle's doings, it turned out that he had been well-established before her arrival in town and the history had been told to her.

Because she had been so kind, and I thought I must have delayed her so near closing time, I bought some cards printed with images of jomon pottery and designs for ceremonial robes. I caught the next bus back home.

Walking up between the plum trees to the steps, and before catching sight of my uncle, I experienced again a rush of joy.

'You never found it for me.'

'The plate?'

He looked puzzled.

'The recipe, your aunt's cake. It doesn't matter.'

'I can make something else.'

'Umnh.'

I sat down.

'What about the plate, though?'

'Well, you may be right about there being four. I was – clumsy, in some ways, back then.'

'Were they really antique?'

'Good copies,' he said. 'Old, not the – goodness, I wouldn't shove the real ones away like that.'

'What would you do? Would you put them in a room in the castle?'

He looked out at the mountains.

'I did have an idea once. Years ago. Doesn't matter now.'

I soaked this in but didn't pursue it.

'Have you telephoned your parents?'

'Not for a few days.'

He pondered this.

'You maybe should,' he sighed. 'Go and make some tea. Bring it out here.'

As we drank the tea, my uncle told me an odd story about a friend of his who found a stray kitten, starving, and took it home. There was a rabbit in his house that had had some babies and lost most of them. The kitten was successfully adopted by the rabbit; and his friend told him, he said, that the cat behaved like a rabbit, though he didn't say how. In any case, they all seemed very happy.

'Does the cat ever seem puzzled by its own impulses? As if it knows it isn't quite like the rabbits?'

Uncle seemed irritated, and the guard went back up.

'How should I know? I'm not a rabbit analyst.'

A few minutes later he told me to get practising. He would stay outside and give me privacy; though if I needed privacy to play and sing, how would I give concerts? From the bottom of a well?

Although the allusion shook me, I decided it was a joke and went in determined to play well. Eventually I was lost, at first in concentration and struggle, then in the music itself.

'Now, out here. Come on. Try out here.'

The music hung in the still air. My voice grew to meet the space.

'It's a change to hear the traditional songs. You're not too bad. Getting it back … It's supposed to be unconscious. Relax.'

He listened again.

'Ah, now you're not standing in the way. That's the song. Not so bad now.'

This was the best conversation we had ever had.

'Where do I get it from, then, the artistic streak?'

He looked annoyed and stood up.

'I said I'd meet a few friends for a drink. Will you be all right? Don't leave the flat. I don't want to find you in a sobbing heap in the haunted tower.' He paused. 'Look at your face! For your information, there are no ghosts of ancient times wandering here. Your aunt used to do the lockup by herself when I was working.'

I only practised a little more after he had gone and

distracted myself with the television after that. I helped myself to a little food and some sweet crackers and fruit. I telephoned my parents.

'Are you getting along with Uncle?' my mother asked. 'He can be a little withdrawn. He's quite thoughtful, though, in the practical sense.'

'He made me practise tonight. He was quite nice about it.'

'No flattery, I hope. No, that wouldn't be like him. Have you made any young friends?'

I had not; at least, not to mix with outside work.

'Mum – just a thing – that flower vase.'

'Which one?' Mother had too much pottery, but not much was so good; a lot came from department stores.

'The sharp-looking one with – like a sculpture with the – painting on the different planes.'

'Honestly, I've no idea. Why? You're not about to tell me you broke it before you left? I haven't seen it for a while.'

'No, no, no of course not. The wedding present one – no. I just wondered who gave it you.'

'Well, that would be your uncle and aunt, more Auntie really. Why?'

'And … who made it? Was it a famous – would I be able to get you something to go with it?'

'I don't think he's still around, dear. Not for ages. Look, have a word with your father. My ladies are starting to arrive.'

'Hello, hello, yes, I'll be escaping soon, your mum's busy. I'll be off out, leave them in peace. How are things? Are they pleased with you still? Not the new girl now, eh?'

'It's all right.'

'It will be better than all right if you make up your mind what you are going to do. Not half thinking you could be a star. What sort of a plan is that? Be practical. Are you helping Uncle? Give him my best. I've got a book he might like, brain puzzles, keep him sharp. I'm really getting into them. When we come up, we'll bring it.'

'Oh, are you coming up?'

'We thought we'd have a trip. You can take us to your favourite eating place. Your mum would like to see some big shops too. Not that she needs anything.'

'Well, I've only really been to a ceramics gallery, but near closing time. I think there's a café there – a good one, I mean – and it's near a park. I don't go out after work.'

'Don't let your mum near any more ceramics. Have you made any friends? It's not right, having no fun.'

'All the other teachers are old, and married.'

'What a shame. What about the – the, er – pupils, the – group members? Try. Try to make friends.'

'Dad, I'm in charge. I can't be friends with them.'

We both paused.

'Will you tell me when you're coming up?'

'We were discussing that. I suggested just coming to the station and hoping you'd happen by, but your funny mum thought we'd organise a hotel and ring Uncle to meet somewhere. Odd woman, no sense of adventure.'

'What was Auntie like? Was she like Mum?'

'Look, she and your mum were close. Why not ask her? Not on the telephone. Properly, when we come up. Try to find a restaurant. Ask your uncle, he'll be in with all the good businesses. You arrange it, though, don't leave it to him. Not that pottery place. A proper restaurant.'

I promised to ask and we ended the call.

Somehow, the flat seemed neither too sparse, nor was I too aware of the vast spaces outside it. It was like any bachelor's flat, although my uncle had been married. I decided I could watch a film. I found only an old melodrama, in black and white, which I thought might be fun. There was sweeping orchestration, lots of rain, and a forced marriage to the local lord, even though the heroine loved a penniless artist. The local lord, observing a tryst – a perfectly innocent one, but desperate with longing – from his tower, lured the artist into a trap and seemed to do away with him. However, he escaped the dungeon just as the water rose, and ran – very fast – up the steps and into the courtyard, where he was too late to save his beloved – who thought him dead – from jumping down the well. He followed her.

I turned cold.

This was just an old film. Why did it shake me and disturb my happier mood?

Some rustling behind me made me start.

'I remember this.' My uncle had come in quietly and stood musing. 'We were enthralled by films like this – believed every moment, though, personally, I liked battle scenes best. Funny, how silly it all looks now. What's up? You don't get worked up over an old film, do you? There are worse things in real life, but we have to deal with them. I hope you don't get so upset when one of you plays a wrong note.' He sat down. 'Of course, even the battle scenes weren't convincing. It was all a bit too clean. Ha. Worst are the films without any suffering at all. All rosy and lovely, then people get the idea – no. Life's not … I brought you a beer. No work tomorrow, go on.'

He only poured me half, and took the rest himself.

'Oh, I did ring Mum and Dad, they want to come up and visit. Dad wondered about a meal somewhere.'

'Umnh.' Uncle nodded.

'It must be a long time since you met up.'

'Families aren't all over each other these days. We know where we are if there's need.'

'Yes, but … Did you ever visit us when I was small? Because I can't remember, and – well – I've never been here before. I wondered why.'

He regarded me for some moments.

'Is there anything else on? What about a game show? They're good for a laugh before turning in. Come on, drink up.'

After the game show, which was not funny and didn't make sense to me, Uncle sent me abruptly to bed, and I heard him on the telephone for a long time, in his room.

That night, the film I had watched mingled with repeated scenes from my other dreams: the joyful walk through the gallery, the moonlight in the well and the shattered plate turning, turning on the surface of the water; my uncle ordering me to search, the well cover in his arms, and the young man hiding behind a willow in the garden, a willow that he was painting even as he hid behind it. I turned toward the castle, trying to find my way to the steps, to see my uncle in his familiar, less threatening guise. Instead of the castle, the steps led to an angular porcelain sculpture, the facets painted with broken scenes; nowhere could I see the whole design. People I felt I should have known were talking in everyday tones about ordinary matters, but they were strangers to me and I had no answers. There was no danger to me, but something had intentions that I couldn't name.

This time I woke slowly, gradually regaining control of my thoughts. I was up before my uncle and started to prepare breakfast. He was mildly gratified when he saw my efforts and told me that my parents would be up that day, which was a great surprise. I always expect a run-up to every event.

We met my parents, who were in smart clothes, looking like pictures of themselves, and had a meal in a private room of a restaurant owned by Uncle's old friend. Dad looked at me with raised eyebrows, but didn't ask who had made the arrangements. Afterwards, we went to the superior department store, where Uncle enjoyed the attentions of those who recalled his days in management, and ran into a few other friends shopping for gifts or clothes. He introduced us; we exchanged pleasantries and afterwards went back to the castle.

I was asked to play and sing, which I did. Afterwards I went to prepare a little tea, and found the plates, four of them, and a cake ready to serve. My mother turned the plate in her hand, as the pieces had turned in my dream, and looked around the room.

Uncle said, 'I find it easier to keep without a lot of things about.'

Mum said, 'So austere, though.' She looked at the tea-plate. 'She had a gift, you know.'

Uncle's expression didn't change.

Dad said, 'So many do. I'm not sure she was so out of the ordinary. The illusion of moonlight on water, whether you do it with a brush or strings and song, is nothing more than technique. I'd say that the greatest talents are the people with the toughest minds. It's not magic. If you're made of porcelain, you break.'

'Auntie painted the flower vase too, dear,' my mum rushed

in, 'but gave up when she married your uncle. Very happy they were, too, after she took to the castle, and – got on with making the business work here.'

She stopped suddenly. There was a pause. Had she forgotten the next part of her speech?

'She shouldn't have given up,' I said. My voice came out through my teeth, sounding strange.

Uncle looked at my dad.

'I'm glad you came,' he said to Mum. 'It's been too long. We talked about coming up to see you after you wrote, but then … she was ill again.' And to me: 'Your aunt had times when she found life very hard. Most of the time she was on top of everything, but then … People never guessed. She just stayed in here. We managed.'

'It was her decision to stop painting. I told her it was a suitable hobby for the long evenings, for a lady in her position,' Mum said. 'But she just stopped.'

Dad leaned forward.

'Uncle cared for your auntie. He did the best he knew at the time.' He glanced at Mum.

Uncle said, 'I was not your auntie's gaoler. Listen – no, it's time. I had a good friend, an artist. His people made fine porcelain, very traditional, but he had big ideas. For a while he taught your aunt, and – this was when we were young, very young. He – well, I suppose all of us – we were talking about living wild in the mountains, restoring some ruins and building kilns. He gave Auntie the idea that she was some kind of inspiration, had – I don't know why – some special talent. It – we'd just been married, not long at all, and I'd settled to the job, you know. It was a dream, but I knew that's all it was, people don't.'

He stopped. No one moved.

'Was there a quarrel?'

I'm sure I spoke out loud, but everyone was looking at Uncle, and he just carried on. My mind had raced along as he had spoken, painting in details as though I were watching a film. I imagined a profound love between the married aunt, her talents suppressed by the diligent, unromantic husband, and the handsome man in the photograph. I saw her, head bent over one of his sculptural pieces, using a fine brush to paint a broken scene, a message –

Uncle exhaled heavily.

'We were planning an exhibition, here. A collaboration. I saw no harm in that. The family approved.'

I imagined the artist and the young wife, walking between the plum trees, talking of poetry, art and death, planning their exhibition, always avoiding the declaration that was brimming in the air.

My mother spoke.

'The more you talk, the less you tell. The details don't matter. Listen. The exhibition was cancelled when your aunt found that she was going to have a baby.'

Again, my own imagination wrote the script, swift and complete: whose was the child?

'We disagreed. I accused my friend of giving my wife ridiculous ambitions, and of wearing her out when she needed to conserve her strength. In the end he went off somewhere and we lost touch. Your aunt was fragile. I knew that. He didn't. One evening, near the end of her pregnancy, she accidentally broke one of the antique dishes. Well, she took it into her head that she had to pay. So most of the work she'd done, she took out to the well and dropped it in –'

'All the little moons –' I whispered.

'The tea plates. Well, I stopped her, It was – there was no call for that, not at all. Fortunately we'd filled in the well up to a safe height. I could clear up, you see. She ... she did like the baby, when it was born, but – she couldn't cope. Mentally or physically. She was – hectic. One day she broke her wrist doing some needless job, her own parents were out –'

Dad interrupted.

'So we took on the baby. Gave you the peace you needed to care for –'

'Just a minute! Where's the child now?'

Was I the child? I thought, and waited to be told. They exchanged glances; I could feel them choosing words, signalling for a spokesman.

'He developed problems. When we knew you were on the way, we had to find a special, properly-equipped place for him. Your aunt thought we'd let him down.'

'Did he – did I ever come here? Did I meet him?'

Laughing children in the castle; hide and seek.

'No. As I said, we started looking after him, then he was in the home, and – then he died, and you were born.'

Uncle was listening, gazing at the past.

Mum said, 'The important thing is, we're back in touch. A family again. It's a pity we let things go for so long, but there's no need to dig things up now. We've told you, and that's it.'

Dad said, 'In a way, it's quite an ordinary story. A sad one, but just life, you know.'

Uncle spoke.

'Your aunt was perfectly able, you understand, once she settled down. She accepted what had happened with her son.' He stood up. 'So now you know,' he said, 'so no more mystery, and no more questions. It's just life.' Then to my parents: 'Now, will you take a final drink before I call your taxi?'

As my parents chatted quietly and prepared to leave for their hotel, I watched them but I could not be drawn in. They were deeper than I had known, and I might drown in their secrets. Yet, I reasoned, why should they not be? They were not merely my parents. My uncle had said there were no more questions, but I had been told everything and nothing. He was simply forbidding further inquiry, putting the lid firmly on the past and trapping its echoes, its shards, where no light could penetrate.

A month later I was on the train back to the village. My visit and my work at the school were over. The castle had become familiar and its dimensions unthreatening. There were no more dreams. I was still brimming yet tongue-tied, and not simply because my elders had, in their own way, closed the subject. All my life I had found myself burdened, yet unable to speak about anything important. Where the spirit to challenge my uncle had come from I had no idea, because I was not usually forthright. He was reserved, but not hostile, and most of the time he behaved as though I was not there. All the events and dreams were stirred and merged, until, when the time came to leave, I had provided myself with an explanation for my experiences.

Memory is a strange possession, and we are not its captain.

I wondered, as we rattled through the countryside, about the hidden drawer in the great chest in my dream, which I had not been able to open. Perhaps it signified that I would never know.

I opened my lacquer lunch box, relishing the prospect of

swaying along as I nibbled at the contents like a little white rabbit, watching the view change; my own private picture show. We stopped at a country station and one passenger stood waiting. I put my fingers to my mouth because, just as I had popped a whole seaweed cracker into my mouth to stop it crumbling, he had looked directly into my eyes.

He was well down the carriages as he boarded, so I felt safe from intrusion. A few moments later, he arrived. He sat opposite. A little further along there was an elderly couple, making occasional remarks and grunts of agreement, sharing their lunch. I felt safe knowing they were there.

The man made a remark to his wife, who turned and said 'Aaah', softly, before smiling kindly at me with a kind of bow. I thought she must believe I was someone else, so I tried to smile, then looked away.

The young man opposite took in a breath. Words queued up behind his teeth till he had my attention.

'Forgive me, but I recognised you. I suppose you're on your way home. Do you know me?'

I looked at him, because I had to, but it felt impolite. Was he the man my aunt had loved? The man for whom she had flown, arms spread and sleeves a-flutter, down the well, following the precious discs of moonlight? He was different. In the photograph his chin was wrong, his eyes sardonic. Now, he looked – how could I say? Cautiously kind. He leaned forward.

'I am Maro.'

Whom else should you be but yourself? I thought. My own name meant excellence, but my parents should have named me differently.

He was talking again, explaining that he had a friend in the village the train had stopped at, but why should I care about that? He said that he had been impressed by my contribution to the music group. He puzzled me. Why was he talking about his work and the healing power of music? I wanted to hear about the child, the child I had played with in the castle, the others who had screamed and run ... His child, and the child of my mother's sister, the fragile aunt by blood.

He sat back, serenely gazing out of the window, but still with me, as though not talking was part of the conversation. The past receded; my aunt was not drowned but died in a hospital, an old lady; no, he was lying. So was my uncle.

The man who called himself Maro excused himself and made a call. He asked what I was going to do when I arrived.

'I'm being met,' I said, cautiously.

He seemed to know already; but then, as he was dead, or old elsewhere, on some mountain, sending his shade to look after me, of course he would know.

I know things too.

It was good to be home. My bed, with its row of soft rabbits and cats and the posters from my Academy concert on the wall. My parents, forcing me to teach people who were not even music scholars, who could only clap their hands or blow a little flute, thought they knew best. I had always been asked to play at the end of each day. It had been wonderful. The little classroom echoed until the curtain descended and they brought me such flowers. One man gave me a flowering plum tree; he was my aunt's lover, who always asked me for a little square of cake.

There are some people, though, who understand. My

mentor at the Academy came to tea, and on another occasion my mother's flower group listened, listened in the litter of petals and stalks on her table, forgetting their arrangements to be lost in mine, in mine, in mine. They smiled, taking my hand; more than one looked long and wisely into my eyes, and remarked to my mother, as they left:

'Such a gift. So gifted. So sad. So very sad.'

Talespin

There was a long silence.

'Well that's cheery, I must say. Nothing like a happy ending, and that.'

A bearded Tale held up its misty hand and indicated, 'Hush'.

'Pardon me for living ... which, I may say, is a sight more than –'

The gaudy Ellafella was quieted, simply by the others' silence.

'Is this, indeed, a happy ending?'

If the student had met her destiny, she was fulfilling her purpose; happiness is as changeable as the play of light on water. The Tales debated long into the night until all that could be heard was the snoring of Ellafella, and all that could be seen was the glint of moonlight on the tinsel around Ellafella's collar as the breathing rose and fell.

'What's that one's purpose, I wonder?'

'Lost, I'm afraid. Or changed beyond belief. It's true enough that those more popular Tales are still in the world, but – such a distorted, mutant version, lacking all truth. One must pity such.'

'Are we pure and unchanged, then?'

The older Tale considered.

'We preserve our deepest core truths, and our – those of us with a humorous twist – the flavour of that fun, yet … where were we born? I always believed myself to be a European Tale, but I found an Indian coin in the folds of my robe …'

'Can you hear that? Is it one of us?'

'Yes, of course. No – no, it seems to be … a human voice. Don't be afraid. It can't harm you. Listen. Which of us is this intruder going to Tell?'

Rawhead and Bloody Bones

Visiting my mother –

'It doesn't start like that!'

'Hush. Listen …'

Visiting my mother, but from a different starting place, in a region I loved and thought I knew, I took a wrong exit from an island on a widened road that used to be a lane. Turn your back for thirty years and it's all chaos when you return. We had visited often, but not from this particular location, and that made all the difference.

It made the difference of a county border.

Stubbornly pressing on, instead of turning back, the car brought me into a curtain of mist and on to haunted Pendle Hill. In Lancashire. I drove past a few cottages, braced and with their heels stuck in to avoid sliding downhill, my progress watched by their stony-faced inhabitants.

Eventually I saw a sign marking the road to Haworth. I knew I could find my way from the Worth to the Wharfe valley, so I pushed on across the moor. One mile of land but six of road; and one house, or at least a chimneyed roof, by the side of a tarn with wind-whipped water lapping the reeds, sparked a memory.

I recalled my grandmother, Nanny Burns, in her red Hillman Imp, bouncing and lurching over the moorland lanes, running the car into the bank after an encounter with a sheep.

'It were a herd of cows, what a tale, you do talk –'

A herd of skittish cows, then, driven by a dog and a distracted lad, had made her mount the bank, and after they had passed by she couldn't start the car. Climbing out, she stood in her shoes and wondered; until, catching sight of a roof, she reckoned there must be a house under it and picked her way down the slope. Around the end gable, by the drystone wall, a hawthorn hung with three dead crows, twirling like musical box ballerinas. A pile of tractor tyres and a series of stone troughs, white sinks and pots guarded the wooden porch. Shortly a woman came and let Nanny into the porch to tell her tale. As she spoke, Nanny noticed a shadow grow and shrink across the wall behind the woman, and a door closed; so when she was invited to wait inside, she expected to meet, perhaps, the woman's husband. But there was no one in the room except a dog in a basket by the unlit range.

Perched on a lumpy chair, Nanny saw that the dog was, in fact, a pig; but it was quiet enough. She gazed around the room; above a bookcase in the shadows was a glass case with a stuffed fox lacking its brush; beside the opposite chair, a knitting bag trailed wool on to the rug, and there was a piano accordion case with rusted catch by the dog basket. The air was close, with a mingling of green and mildewed smells she didn't know she liked.

The farm lady came in, told her shortly that she'd be right enough to get to town, no damage, and advised her to take care in her "unsuitable" court shoes.

'Well, I never wanted to go tramping on the moor, I were driving.'

The last odd thing she saw by the road was a dead badger, its clawless paws bound round with heather sprigs, before she was away over the hills to home.

Inside the farmhouse, Elsie clicked her tongue and the pig jumped up out of his basket to sit up in the chair opposite her own. She picked up her knitting and nodded toward the piano accordion. Elsie liked a bit of music in the afternoon.

Everyone came to Elsie's stall on the market to buy her remedies, but they were wary of her, too. They would chatter away with the Broken Biscuit Man and be confiding with the Corset Lady, but with Elsie they were respectful but brief. Her pig – named Cyril after her departed spouse – sat in the back of her stall and travelled home with her on the tractor, a noisy little vehicle with a home-built trailer on the back.

There were rumours regarding Elsie and her powers. Though she was unkind to none, she never smiled but with a sideways glint. She had no gossip and never joked, but seemed to command attention simply by standing still. The men said that life was all work for Elsie, and no wonder she was strange. The women, some of them, said she was a witch, a heavy word in those parts; others that she was a Wise Woman. And those that had any reason to call on her at twilight – to deliver something, perhaps, or check on her welfare in the snowed-in months – reported hearing a gruff, snuffly voice singing or chatting with Elsie, and of seeing something like the silhouette of her husband, a portly man, in his cap and with his pipe, rippling on the drawn curtain, playing on his old accordion but with the strangest, longest snouty profile – distorted no doubt by the folds of thin brocade.

Someone claimed it was Cyril, the pig. He rooted about in the compost where Elsie chucked her herbs and old remedy-water. He must have scrobbled up a lexicon of power in all those mixings.

'She'll not be lonely, then,' was one remark, from a woman unmoved by hints of magic.

One day, Elsie arrived at the market without Cyril. The Broken Biscuit Man asked, and the Corset Lady was eventually told, that Cyril had failed to return after his evening wander. When Broken Biscuits tried to joke about a sow in the next farm, Corset Lady hushed him and took Elsie for a cup of tea in the Market Hall café.

'He'll be waiting for thee tonight, love, don't you fret.'

Cyril was not waiting that night, or the next.

Before the following dawn, Elsie sat in her chair, despairing, her eyes fixed for a full hour on a Book that lay sideways on the top shelf. She was the guardian of that Book, sworn never to use it, as her mother had sworn; now, she took the low stool from under her feet and jumped up on it. The heavy Book, torn free of its spiderweb wrappings, almost upset the stool and Elsie as she dragged and clutched it to her. When she opened it, the spine cracked and something seemed to exhale.

Being busy was a cure for melancholy often sold by Elsie on her stall, along with the herbs she instructed customers to plant at two mile intervals on windy days across the moor, keeping one sprig only to keep beneath their pillow. Sleeping with the sprig, they said, cured their mood wonderfully; though the magic never worked a second time when they had stayed indoors.

Elsie filled an enamel bowl with water, ran into the yard to pluck herbs, and used a paper spill from the jug on the mantel to light the gas. She struggled to chop and throw in the herbs in the right order, at the right time, peering at the ancient writing between each addition; but at last the steam rose and she read the spell.

Swirling, changing colour, the steam dissipated, exposing a shaky vision of a greasy, painted wall. Elsie tapped the bowl, widening the picture, until she could see a table spread with newspaper, an overflowing ashtray and a dish. A man sat eating from a plate hidden from Elsie by the dish, and he slouched low over his meal. Soon, he threw a thin thing into the dish, slurped up some mashed potato, and then picked up something and began to gnaw; something pale and tender; something fringed with crisp, brown edges, which made him close his eyes in relish; something which left him holding a thin, white bone, which he cast into the dish.

The wall behind him seemed to melt, exposing the yard behind his house, where even in winter flies buzzed and feasted; in the corner lay a pile of bones, and above them, on a hook, hung the head and face of her friend Cyril.

The picture vanished. Trembling, Elsie scattered more herbs, added more water, and looked again at the great Book.

> 'Raw Head and Bloody Bones,
> Ey up, Cyril, get thee home;
> Frame thissen and get on out,
> Nivver pause to laike about.'

This she repeated until the head opened its eyes and began to swing.

Elsie went to work the next day. Corset Lady and Broken Biscuit Man agreed she seemed to be almost herself again, though she took a long lunch break in the Market Hall café. The café was opposite the new butcher's stall. For a full hour Elsie watched the butcher's antics as he tried to charm and cheek the women, stroking back his slick black hair, twirling and knotting sausages with an insolent, stagey air as if it was a magic trick. Elsie looked at the clock.

She packed up early that day, to be home in time. She sat in the parlour and waited.

Because the Book was so old, and un-consulted for a century or more, it had taken some time to warm up. The vision of Cyril's face, eyes closed, beginning to stir, was something like a trailer for a film, or the Flicks as Elsie would have called them. The Book was responding to the Call, but the spell itself, once the job had been identified and terms agreed when Elsie closed the pages, would take a little longer.

When the Butcher left for the market there was no change in the pile of bloody bones, and he winked, clicking his tongue, and even told Cyril's head that he'd be home late as he had an evening planned – first pleasure, then business, and finally a few drinks after hours with his friends.

'So don't wait up, and no nagging when I come rollin' home. Sithee later, Chops.'

As the Butcher's van lurched out of the yard, one of Cyril's eyes opened, unsettling a fat fly.

From the pile of bones a whistling wheeze arose, and Cyril's jaw creaked open as a whisper drifted around:

'See you later.'

As the grey sky darkened into slate, then night, the bones began to shift and slide and stick themselves together. The head swung wildly and squished itself on to the shape of Cyril, and he walked stiffly from the yard.

Out of the town and up to the hills walked Cyril, feeling the breeze more than he used to, and it occurred to him suddenly that he could barely see. Twirling from a warning tree against a gritstone wall there hung a crow with jet eyes bright in death. Cyril scooped them out and, with them in his sockets, he could see all the way home in a straight line.

The road, though, was an up and down and left and right kind of a road, so he went slowly. Now that he had eyes, he noticed that his front legs, swinging like arms, ended suddenly. Just then he stumbled upon a dead badger with wonderful claws. Cyril took the claws, and, feeling sorry for the roadkill, fastened heather sprigs to the clawless paws for grace and dignity in death for his cousin. He even wound them on with some moist, stringy fibres snapped off his own bone ends.

Now Cyril felt more decent, except for his tail. There was a draught, and nothing to twitch. He saw a dead fox by the road and took its brush and jammed it on, and so he went, swinging like a girl with a long ponytail.

Midnight long gone, and Cyril getting into his stride, when a lurching, screeching, motor van rocked over the hill. Cyril stood on the crown of the road and the van braked sharply. The Butcher wound down his window and stuck his head out.

'That Bert? Want a lift?'

Cyril moved into the glare of the headlights, and the Butcher realised that this was not Bert. He gulped.

'Who are you?'

'Your last meal.'

The crow's black eyes shone.

'What you got them eyes for?'

'To see your grave.'

The responses given should have encouraged the Butcher to drive off as quickly as he could, but he continued the interview. Perhaps horror paralysed him. Perhaps it was the drink. It's easy to criticize when you've never encountered a skeletal hog with crow's eyes behaving in a threatening manner on the highway, and there is no etiquette, as far as I know, for this situation.

Curiosity prompted the Butcher again, or perhaps he hoped to play for time and make his escape.

'What you got them claws for?'

'To dig your grave.'

Now the Butcher was weak and only managed to whisper, 'What you got that tail for?'

'To sweep your grave.'

Cyril leaned into the window.

'Right then,' he said, 'I always believe in returning a courtesy, don't you? Only right and proper. I was your dinner last night. Now, I'm fair clemmed with hunger, I can see my ribs. So. Are you ready?'

This was a rhetorical question, and any answer the Butcher tried to give failed to persuade Cyril, sounding, as it did, like a strangled scream.

The moorlands carried on their midnight business, unconcerned.

Talespin

The Tales sat around the fire, seeing each other in the flames; a log split, shooting sparks on to the rug, and the Tales watched as each spark became a glowing orange pony. Stampeding together on the hard earth, only calming as they cooled to black, they grazed on moss.

'What were real people doing in the story? Are you going to let them twist you about like this?'

'I don't know, and that's a fact. What you all don't seem to grasp, we just get put out there. I don't got no say in what they do to me. I always felt kinda swampy and hung with Spanish moss, myself, but I can't recall no further back than about –'

'The main thing being: do you retain your essence?'

Two of the Tales began arguing about authenticity. The pre-Christian saga, usually told in high style at niche History Festivals, claimed that urban legends were cheap modern fakes, with none of the significance of the true Folk Tale.

'If folk are tellin' 'em, they are Folk Tales, you bletherer. Just 'cos your lot capered about in skins, you reckon to be better than them. I like 'em, and the shaggy dog stories too.'

There was a grateful 'Wuff' from somewhere.

'There's no message, or *echo*, in the urban myths, they are merely ... Nobody could take them seriously.'

'For example? What are you about?'

Ellafella considered.

'Well, being nice, and beautiful, and getting the prince and a happy ending.'

'No!'

'Well of course there is the villainess and her daughters, ugly as sin and just plain nasty, but funny as well –'

'No, no, you see, you've lost your way; it's about death in childbirth and the insecurity of the second wife, the fear of destitution; and the ugliness probably relates more to the deprivation than actual physical – although that's a moot point, why beauty is always such a big deal ...'

There was a pause.

'Death and desperation. That'd go down a treat at Newark Empire second house. Just squeeze it in between the kitchen scene and the front of cloth sweet-chucking. I'm viable, I am. People still know me. Where were you when I found you? You can be as meaningful as you like, but if nobody knows you, guess what, Sunshine, you just don't count.'

Before the Tales had time to respond, a shadow fell across them all. Lifting his pointed feet, stepping over their heads with scarcely a wobble and folding himself up nearer the fire, was a thin Tale of impressive height. His lower limbs were sunburnt, wearing shorts, but his hair was a crown of crystal, his breath an icy blade.

As he warmed himself, the icicles melted and made a rushing stream that would have quenched the fire if he had not bent down and drunk it up. When he sat up again, his drenched hair hung like a curtain of brass, so he tossed back his head and caught three of the Tales behind him with the spray. From the purse at his belt he took a folded paper bird, which he gallantly presented to the Tale just told, who took it gently and would have put in into the folds of her shawl; but it seized her and put her on its back, growing all the while, and flew off with her.

'Allow me to introduce –'

'Oh, we know who you are. Try to make yourself scarce.'

'Every word I say is true, and there's truth in everything my subjects do.'

'Oh yes. Such as your shape shifters. Look, I've nothing against magical or amazing deeds, I have a few of those – monsters too – but they don't defy the logic or the purpose of my message. Basically, my monsters are symbolic, as are the –'

'Are you a Tale or a pedant? No wonder we were neglected. Shape shifting? You don't believe in that?'

'Demonstrate. Show us what you mean.'

Captain Raven and the Sun

Jim the Park Keeper was enjoying his tea-break in the dark little hut, dense with the smells of earth and creosote. He had begun dipping a biscuit into his tea, just enough to soften the chocolate, when a hullabaloo beyond the door made him jump. He glanced at the clock, let his biscuit sink into the tea and snatched up his cap.

Just beyond the Busy Lizzies, two scallywags in long grey shorts and concertina socks danced and jeered, their backs to Jim. Instantly, they found themselves brandished, feet dangling, as Jim gave them a shake.

'Don't you pair of I-dunno-whats ever let me catch you again. I know your mothers and I'll be havin' words.'

Spinning slowly from his collar, the bigger boy tried cheek.

'Gerr – 's only Old Man Raven.'

Jim gazed across the park at the tall figure shambling, hands deep in pockets, black coat flapping around his shins and hat pulled low.

'That gentleman there, you owe him. We all do.'

'Gerr – what you on about?'

'Look! What's that up there?'

They squinted.

'The sun, innit.'

'Well, let me tell you boys, if it wasn't for that gentleman there –' He swung the boys to look, but a Green Line bus obscured the view. 'That up there ...' waggling the boys toward the sun, 'woulden be up there, and you woulden be able to play in the park, 'cos the park would be dark.'

Four huge eyes gazed up at him, and the older boy tried a feeble, 'Gerr –', but curiosity stopped it.

'Right, you two. Sit on that roller. Mind the handle and sit still. Now listen.'

No one could recall the days before the Great Tyrant, Tupilac, had lifted his arm against the land. Nobody knew, as they stumbled home before curfew, who would be missed in the morning, or upon what charge. Their only joy was that lightening of the heart when, in the broken pavings, a violet might be glimpsed, valiantly striving and purple with effort; or when the shoots of vegetables, planted in old sinks and buckets by the door, shone emerald-bright like hope.

Tupilac saw this hope, or someone told him. A people without hope can be more easily controlled.

One morning, the citizens awoke to find it was Night.

Alarm clocks rang in dawnless rooms; candles were lit for the breakfast, and dull-eyed citizens ventured into morning streets pitch as midnight, the air dark as peat.

Before too many days, the people yawned and blinked, bowing their shoulders all around the clock. They grew numb, uncertain. None were inspired. None would rise against the Tyrant.

Captain Raven, of the Special Secret Division First Class, stood in the office of his Underground Mission HQ. His superior regarded him.

'Deuced if I want you to go, Raven. I don't claim to understand your methods, but you're damned useful here on the ground. Still, no denying you can fly. It's a dangerous mission, Raven.'

A long pause.

'If you think you know where it is – and I'm foxed – get it back, Raven, before the dark and the cold overwhelm the people. Of course, Tupilac's at the bottom of it. No call for active tyranny when there's neither light nor warmth. All right. You're on the mission. Good luck, Raven. Come back in one piece.'

In the early morning dark, Raven climbed into his crate. The lightweight plane swooped up toward the clouds.

Piercing the clouds, the aeroplane vanished, not hidden by the vapour but merging with it, becoming cloud itself, along with Raven, master of disguise. The cloud rose until the air became intolerable for its constitution, then suddenly compressed itself to a speck of stardust smaller than a gnat could dance on. The stardust, spinning upwards, was a glinting, swinging speck, full of an exultant vigour that almost burst from Raven, but he set his jaw grimly; now was no time to drop his guard and give the game away.

For there, spinning slowly in the starless dark, was the dim grey square of Tupilac's house.

Raven the stardust speck blew against the window glass and looked. In the little room, by dim candlelight, Tupilac sat with his daughter at a great oak table, rough-hewn and rooted to the floor. They chatted idly until Tupilac indicated the iron-bound chest against the wall. His daughter opened the lid, just an inch; there came a fuzzy, buzzing glow of gold, and Tupilac's daughter, with thumb, finger and a delicate twist, pulled a little of the yellow haze from the chest, unravelling it as she crossed the room.

So there they sat, playing with that one ray of the imprisoned sun. Tupilac, he twisted and tore little pieces of the gold, stamped them with his fist, piled them into a tower of coins. His daughter draped her shoulders, twisted a length around her body like a shining evening gown. When they tired of their game, Tupilac commanded his girl to haul in the brightness. As she stuffed the ray back into the chest, the brow of the sun bobbed up, so she slammed the lid, and a little ribbon of torn sunlight wriggled on the floor. They put it on the table, where it gleamed upon the cruel profile of Tupilac.

Raven drifted from the window, down, down toward the clouds, where he, as cloud, descended till the 'plane, Raven inside, dropped on to the airfield.

He lay long musing that night. By morning, he had made his plan.

Tupilac owned all of the ruined buildings in the town. He wanted the basements, the cellars, the long underground passages. One of these basements was too far from other ruins to be effective for transportation or secret abductions, so he had established a night-club. His officers were the patrons; the staff and entertainers, unwilling volunteers or hard-nosed survivors.

One such was Jacques d'Or le Plume, an elegant lounge singer, whose melting eyes and voice had captivated Tupilac's daughter, who sat by the stage each night, two glasses ready. The singer knew of her intent, which he feared; he feared also to disobey, he feared accusations; he lived in fear, which put an alluring tremble into his low notes, inflaming Tupilac's daughter's interest further. Strange and wonderful she found it; then, on the evening when, shyly at first, Jacques gazed into the girl's eyes, seemed unable to desist. As he left the stage she beckoned him and he joined her. Before long, she had invited him to her cosy flat at the back of the club. She sat him in the deep square sofa, whilst she, striking willowy poses, switched on dim lamps around the room.

'No windows, you see. So soft and cosy.' On a pedestal table of stacked green glass, she poured two glasses of champagne. 'You know, you really are something else.' She giggled.

'I know,' he said.

She bent to kiss him briefly, then went to change into something more comfortable. When she returned, the room was empty. Disappointed at first, she promised herself that although Jacques had fled this time, she would win him; poor thing, perhaps she had been hasty.

She sipped the first glass, glancing idly through a magazine, but a sullen, reckless mood seized her, and she stood by the table to drain the second in a gulp. That drink was so much livelier than the first; the bubbles so much more hilarious. One danced across the full bow of her lip, buzzed along the roof of her mouth, danced sparkily down her throat, and down.

There was a crash; tiles of green glass lay scattered on the rug, and the table top was split. Tupilac's daughter heard a sheer satin squeal, felt a cold draught and, looking down, saw what it was that had thrown the table down, what it was that had torn the oyster satin of her once loose negligée.

It was the great, taut peach of her belly.

She fled to her father's house.

'What have you done?' he thundered.

'Nothing.'

'Nothing! Nothing comes of nothing,' bawled Tupilac, and his words spun out into the velvet dark, down to earth, where for a thousand years they blew about; until they alighted on a dandelion clock, which blew into the ear of a Warwickshire playwright, who put them into another angry father's mouth.

Tupilac's daughter was dismayed to have garnered a harvest with no delightful sowing, but despite living in a spinning house above the moon, and having witnessed wonders, Tupilac did not believe her.

Jacques d'Or le Plume rested after his one night spent quietly at home on the instructions of a mysterious stranger. On his return to the Club, was relieved to find that Tupilac's daughter was nowhere to be seen.

Where was Captain Raven?

In the back room of Tupilac's house his daughter lay chin-deep, her belly like the rising moon above the water in a pool carved from rock. She was alone when the red swirled like smoke in the water; alone as her belly collapsed and she caught the little creature she had birthed. In that moment, she was shaken by an overwhelming love. It was the first and purest of her life. When Tupilac returned, his daughter was suckling, with a soft look in her eyes.

For a few days they enjoyed the baby, commenting on his spiky black hair and bright eyes, until the crying began. The cry was rasping, loud and ceaseless. The baby was clean, fed and warm, but quiet only for moments; just as they eased into sleep, Tupilac and daughter were wrenched awake by squawking.

After a week they were both in a miserable trance, until Tupilac realized that the baby was bored. His grandchild was no ordinary baby.

The lid of the chest was lifted, and a thin ray of sunlight draped across the cot. At first, this warmed and entertained the child. But one day, with Tupilac away, the crying began again. The mother draped the single ray across the child, who smiled at first – but suddenly stretched and screamed, so the mother tugged at the sunlight, covering him with yet more golden heat. She tugged so hard that the sun himself bounced up, and like a balloon bounced on to the cradle.

She screamed in fear that her son would turn to cinder; black he did turn, and glossy, and tall; with two great wings he clasped the sun, flying from the place with a 'Caw'.

Tupilac returned to find the mother kneeling, gazing bereft into the empty cot. One gleaming feather lay upon the pillow.

Captain Raven flew up to the hole in the sky with the hook for the sun, and there he hung him, and there he blazed, and the people were warmed, and so Tupilac was vanquished.

The city prospered, with schools and squares, with public parks, and the sun shines on it all.

Every Saturday on Earth, Old Man Raven walks out from his basement under the railway bridge in his flapping coat and black brimmed hat. Behind the High Street, down a greasy lane, there is a newsagent's shop. When the owner sees Raven approach, he calls his daughter down and retreats into the back parlour, where he sits brooding sullenly by the empty grate. Old Man Raven stands regarding the woman pleasantly, until her hand creeps protectively over her belly or she crosses her arms.

Raven speaks.

'Morning, ducks. Looking lovely this morning, not but what you aren't always a sight to behold. Now, dearie, let me get to my list. Mrs Wilson's stamps, right-o – Mr Goldman's Five Boys chocolate – hand me that National Geographic would you, dear? – Oh, yes, someone was asking … have you got the Sun?'

Talespin

'Where's the moral?'

'There should be a point. Perhaps that's why we're redundant. Too much updating, too much entertainment. What's the moral? I know what I'm about.'

'The great days are done. Where are the quests, the grand adventures … dragons … sward like emeralds, and the white horses cantering … silver towers, flags … all grey now …'

The rusty armoured Tale mumbled himself to slumber.

The other Tales listened to a thought … Was it a Tale, or a human thought?

Under the Hill

When first she worked there, she would tell.

To excite their interest, she put, next to the chipped saucer for tips, an image of her mansion on the hill.

Once, someone asked her, head on one side and in a kindly patronising tone, was it her former place of employment? Had she been a Housekeeper, perhaps, or Head Cook?

'Not my place of employment. Just my place.'

No effort could command her voice to regain its fulsome lilt, and she coughed against her strangled words.

The lady gathered her red handbag, deposited a coin or two and left.

That day, the image, already faded, scorched and flared at the touch of a tormenting ray of sun.

'How'd he get through that liddle 'ole?' she murmured, squinting up at a smeared narrow pane.

The little frame burned her fingers as she fiddled with it, removed the ruined memory, and set it up, empty, in its former position.

Whilst there was no one down here, she might as well mop out. She swished bubbling water at a little spider, and, spitefully, slopped more drenchingly when the creature escaped; but she relented, and using a tissue lifted the balled-up creature on to the window sill.

'Want to be of use, dry this one out.'

There was a girl once, a sweet little student, not local ... A light little voice, somewhere up North, wearing what must have been her school uniform skirt and a home-knit jumper. Before the image was destroyed, the girl had seen it and said:

'What beautiful clouds.' Above the house in the image, and all around its hilltop height, reflected too in the windows and the lake, had been a wilderness of clouds. 'Like another world in the sky. Lakes and mountains.'

'Want to know about it? The house?' the old woman asked the girl.

'Got a lecture. Sorry. I'll remember the clouds, though.'

The photograph had been her last possession, in her hand when the mansion blew away. Now it was gone; and how could she tell them who she had been without the photograph to spark a question? How had she come here, and why so old?

The rumble of traffic from above intensified and the turnstile screeched once, twice and more as homegoing women entered with shopping she would guard, with rings they would remove, prompting her kindly warning. Then, comfortable for their journey, hands moist from the towel or thick with scented cream, they would leave, their heels ringing on the stone steps as they ascended into the upper world. Few spoke to her, more smiled, but some seemed put out by her presence, unsure whether to meet her eye.

At last, the lights were switched off. The man – she had never met him, but he whistled – pulled the lattice gates across and she was alone.

There was a door, lit by a greasy moonbeam, and she pushed through it. She recalled a bed with quilts as warm as love and light as clouds; that, she thought, is where I should be. All those who come would be amazed at what I once enjoyed. Curled like a woodlouse, she sought warmth under one blanket and her outdoor coat.

She took to polishing the silver frame whenever a lady paused at her table, hoping that it might impress, but only disparaging glances were cast. The frame was scorched, a little dented, and spoke not of grandeur but of desolation. It looked like a fake.

One day, it disappeared.

Now she had nothing.

Nothing but the spider, dried out and watchful; spinning, spinning, skittering soundlessly along its gossamer tightropes, or tracking her, running toward her bare feet as she eased into the narrow bed just as the light went out.

Gazing in the flickering sour light at the saucer for tips, she wondered how and where she could spend the coins. And on what?

Why was she never hungry?

She had wanted an orchard, under glass, on that great green hillside, to swell with exotic fruits, flourish scarlet trumpet blossoms and thick, sinuous vines, where heated pipes would outdo the sun's deficiencies in this rigorous climate. It had been her habit always to defy circumstance and general wisdom, to raise one arch eyebrow and lift one corner of her mouth when cautioned, taking the view – expressing it, too – that she was of finer yet stronger stuff and could upturn the world and hang it on a peg if she thought it would look better.

There was on the whole hillside only one solitary white and thorny bush, bent into supplication by the gales from the sea, by the winds from the mountain.

Had she dreamt it?

She scrabbled in her memories, straining to recall the mansion, how she had gained it, but other memories or thoughts intruded ... skipping in shoes too big, no socks, and skinning her knee.

She seemed to be sailing, fishing for a fine bright salmon in the sea of memory, glimpsing and then losing sparkling wonders of the life she thought she'd known. At last a memory surfaced, but instead of the nurture she'd hoped for, here was a grey and bloated thing, light and bobbing, buzzing with flies ...

She recalled a smell of damp and drains, gutters gushing with rain, a man on a ladder hauling a door, shouting at her to go in, to get out of the rain ... but the rain was inside, she said, until he slammed the door against it ... a door above her as she lay gazing.

Whose memory was that?

Whose memory was hers?

Who was she, and was she the same person she had been to begin with?

'I should be ...' she began to speak, and her voice shocked her, ringing against the brown tiles, waking goodness knows what listeners to her presence. She remained silent then, but kept the thoughts along the same theme: indignation, blame, and longing for the disappearing past.

Someone had kidnapped her life, she suddenly decided, and given her this degradation and the foul memories of a different childhood, a despicable, ugly life, one she did not deserve. A changeling.

None had come now for almost a day, and she heard the whistling man. As swiftly as possible she went into the narrow room, finding she longed for it, nervous of the larger space and the row of heavy doors like turned backs.

Strange. That once she had ascended a wide stair into a lofty hall, pillars and plinths casting shadows, vast artworks of the obscure, exclusive kind, a dozen smoky mirrors; and through the doors, long enfilades of open rooms, she had walked alone, untroubled, unlonely, until some servant came or perhaps a guest approached her.

What had happened to them?

She had seemed to see the mansion whirl away and the hillside open and herself fall in ...

It must be that during the work to make the orchard, when the hawthorn, blackthorn, whatever, was uprooted, she had fallen, been struck ... So now she must be unconscious.

Lying on the narrow bed, grateful for the meagre comfort and feeling its proportions now more like an embrace, she wondered about the stranger's memory. The running child in rags, the man blocking the roof with a door ... What kind of roof has a door in it? Who comes in from above?

Well, clearly no one. She had recalled a hovel, a patching of sodden scraps to shiver in. It was not her memory. A little sad thrill ran through her – less a thought than a sensation – for the unknown keeper of such memory. The bowed arthritic collector of sparse coins. Such harsh odours; disinfectant, stinging the eyes, to counteract the earthy smells ...

'Ah, I must be in hospital. I can explain all this to myself and climb back up. They will take me home and I can pay a nurse. I should not be in a public hospital, with such conditions. I am ... I am ...'

She slept.

No sun at the window but only rain on the next morning. The ground too must be saturated, for the quarry-tiled floor was dark as with sweat and there was greening around the corners of the walls. Mopping did nothing. She searched and found abrasive brushes, thick poisons that reddened her shining hands, and folded her coat to kneel and scrub. Someone came in, stepping around her, standing above her to wash and use the hot air drier, which moved her white hair, and said:

'Good job. Well done,' and something rattled in the saucer.

The initial thrill of contempt, the impulse to bite back at the remark, was stopped by the sight of the floor and the wall, which gleamed and glowed, dry, sweet and clean. A few flakes of whitewash were soon swept up.

There were no coins in the saucer, but a little brooch of glass set like a butterfly, with a broken pin. The wings glittered pink, grass green and turquoise translucence, even in the sick light of her prison. It was a brooch to charm a child, a market stall find, not something in a jeweller's; yet it caught her in its wings. Had she seen it, long ago? She set it on the window sill and addressed the lazy sun to come and sparkle on it, if he could be bothered.

At noon, the wall opposite was pooled with colour as the sun shone through the butterfly, and her ladies began to remark on it.

'My ladies? Where'd that come from? Who said "my ladies"?'

Once she had the thought it seemed quite natural, and she began to smile and recognise the ones who came daily and began to add their offerings to the saucer.

By the end of … whatever time had passed, the window sill and any ledge or surface where an object could be tied or balanced was dressed. Someone left a colour supplement and she had used its pages to make fans, until someone had given a little pair of scissors, which she used to snip out paper dolls, holding hands and dancing in a midnight chain, horses who cast their shadows on the tiles; more jewellery, all damaged in some way, demanding ingenuity to make it into something new.

A lady left a jacket once. Folding it over her arm, the old cleaner felt its sumptuous depth, and something in the pattern and the weave – it was not conventional fabric for a jacket – overwhelmed her. She was a child, feet frozen in thin-soled shoes, her hand bonily gripped by that of her mother as they looked up, up at the towering draped figures above them, who gazed sightlessly above their heads. The mannequins were not, as usual, dressed in clothes on sale inside, but draped exotically in bold, deep folds of a dozen different fabrics, brilliantly lit. If her mother's hand had not kept her in the grey street, she would have floated through the glass to join them, the lordly ones whose throng she should belong to, she felt sure.

Her mother always took her, when school broke up for Christmas, and put her to sit in the broom cupboard while she cleaned the powder room, and afterwards to see the big windows all along the street.

The cleaner looked at her knotty hands, spreading the fingers, and recognised them.

The light went out.

When she had groped her way to the bed – which, she found, now had an extra blanket – she heard her own voice, its crystal edges bought and paid for, say 'I am not my mother'. It was a memory, but when she tried to repeat the words aloud, it was her mother's voice.

Surely her mother must be dead by now.

She wept.

That night she dreamt of a place she knew. It was not the mansion; her mother had come to it and walked among the few rooms, stroking the inexpensive fittings, exclaiming at the cord to pull the unlined curtains. She had declared it a palace and herself proud of her girl. Her girl's companion had grimaced at the old woman's stern civility, her scalpel gaze, and after her departure had impersonated her. In the woman's dream now, the two rooms looked inviting, her male companion too tall, too thin; and when she looked up there was a door, a panelled door with peeling paint, bulging under the weight of earth, and the long roots of a thorn tree.

Who enters from above?

In her dream, gazing upward, she felt dry pellets of crumbled soil fall on her face. Her tall companion gazed, discompassionately, offering no help.

She woke, choking, and opened her eyes, brushing away … it must be flakes of whitewash.

Yes, but there was soil too, and her eyes opened to see the door, the same peeling door that her mother had told her about, the door to hold the rain off the roof of a hovel, wishing for her daughter a good man and a sound roof; the door her mother, as a child, had thought might open to a world of simple things. It never worried her, she said, only made her glad her father could climb, and heave, and charm an old door from a rich man's builder. When one door closes, the rain stays out, she said.

Here was the door again.

Someone knocked.

A murmuring of flutelike voices in soft debate, which faded with the image of the door.

The woman found herself well rested, ready for the day's work, somehow undisturbed by her visions. That day, she noticed redness in a lady's eyes, splashed uselessly with water.

'Woss up, ducks?' she heard herself say, and listened to the tale.

When she had given her – perhaps her mother's – rough comfort, the lady went, leaving a token in the saucer. It was a small engagement ring and she had seen it before. She had pawned it on the day of the proposal to buy a red dress to dance in. She procured from her dancing partner an invitation …

So on and on she had progressed, meeting, at some woodland revelry on a great estate, the tall thin man nobody seemed to know; and on the same night, the unambitious heir to a fortune, a shy man of deep interests, on whom, she thought, the wealth was wasted. On their divorce she kept the mansion; three years wed, and easily rid.

Now, she tied the ring up where it would turn and twist and catch the sun, idly wondering – then beginning to fear – what the jilted boy had done with his life. An easy catch, he'd gazed entranced, but was no fool – she hadn't liked his blunter insights or his cautions. Nevertheless, she reasoned that he had a trade, was perhaps susceptible to determined pushing, which would launch him into higher realms and wages. Failing alternative chances, as an only child of modestly comfortable, elderly parents, he would be the heir to a small house, a brown semi- detached in a semi-pleasant suburb between the poor centre and the wealthy green edge of town.

It was on one of the rural walks on which he took her that she had first seen the mansion. A butterfly had landed on her collar. He had joked that the butterfly knew its kin, as she was, he thought, a flittery thinker with no sound plan. That was his mistake.

He'd bought the butterfly brooch-glass, she noted, not even amethyst, but pretty, and she had worn it on the red dress that he never saw.

Had she returned his ring?

Surely she had, it was the decent thing. Perhaps her mother had made her face him, then, until her visit to the dreary flat, hardly spoken, never met … never since that day.

'You are one of us now,' her tall, so tall, companion had told her, in and out of the dance, and the lantern swinging, half-drunk promenade through the unending woods … Had that been on her wedding night?

Her husband had loved his library, but the house was fading. Walls of arsenic green with tarnished gold, a rocking horse bald of mane, and furniture installed two centuries before … except for the kitchen parlour where he sat in an old club chair, the loose covers washed and shrunk to straining, and listened to harp music on his father's radio. She railed at him that she was there, too, and he, uncomplaining, wrote cheques for her to fund a few alterations. When, unsettled by her continual crowds and purchases, he'd spent more time in a quiet literary club than by her side, she had divorced him for neglect, for … What had it been?

She told her tall companion once, when he arrived unexpectedly, as always, of her plans for the orchard. They were standing in the vast glass gable for which five tall mullions had been sacrificed, and he had said a strange thing.

'The mansion is all yours, my dear; but the hill belongs to us.'

Talespin

'Does she get out?'
  None could answer.
  'Who was it? Why didn't you finish?'

The Greek myths, draped over a fallen trunk, began to murmur uncomfortably.

'Although we concede that there are some themes we recognise, we – we don't lay claim to this. In fact, it sounded to us more like your style, hills and trees being assaulted, humans drawn into a throng of dancing revellers …'

There was a long silence.

'Never anything funny about you. Too fond of the old inescapable torments, no way out.'

Tales began hissing, bawling, or pontificating about their merits.

At last, they were exhausted.

'Have you done? Good. Strikes me you're all missing something. What we just got, all on us, wasn't one of us. No.'

Ellafella slewed her gaze across the front row.

'Shall I tell you what it was, boys and girls? Shall I?'

There was an awkward mutter.

'Can't hear you!'

'Yes please.'

'That's better. I have some advantages, being one foot in and one foot out, even if that makes me – what was it – a hybrid monstrosity? That what you said, Gelert? Welsh, are you? Huh. Never mind that. Just have a chat some time with some of your elders. Now, about what we just all heard. Or felt. True, there were some bits, or elements, if you like that better, some bits that we could see ourselves in. It wasn't a Tale, though, so none of us could tell it.'

The crumpled page rustled.

'Perhaps it was a story. Someone – maybe – wrote it.'

'So it can never be altered. Or grow.'

The page seemed to smile.

'Perfection needs no improvement.'

'Think. What are we? Tales. We know that. What are we for? Do we know that? That woman in the story: is she in the world, the human world?'

'She can't be.'

'Think about this. As Tales, we're full of ... ogres and fathers and ... transformations. Tales as told can't talk about themselves, yet here we are. Out in the world, and out of ourselves. What if that woman had got a bit of one of us ... let me think ... caught up in her life?'

'Not one of us. One of the characters we tell of. Out in the world and out of our Telling.'

'That's all we need. If they get out, we'll be empty. It's not humans forgetting we need to watch, it's our ... contents ... leaking out.'

'I warned you, ages ago,' muttered one of the Greek myths. 'You never believed me. Nobody listens. '

'Does she get out? Will you focus on one thing, please?'

'That's a point. You say *does* she get out, not *will* she get out. I keep telling you, she's real. She's out there. Down there. Somewhere ...'

'In their world, such things don't happen. If she exists, she isn't enchanted or imprisoned, not really. In her mind ... we saw her dream, not her life. That's where we –'

'Saw her. Take a bow, love. That's where we live. Truth not facts. Tell you now, I don't know whether she even had a big house. I do know – well, I think – she didn't hear us, never. Not as a child.'

Plough the Road:
a folk tale and a tale from the future

There was famine coming over the hill.

The food from last year's harvest was thinning out, and the fields gave nothing but stones and dry stalks.

In his castle, the king fretted.

He listened to his advisors.

He made a decree.

Four nights later, six young friends sat around a fire in the forest. One, nervous of the long, sick silence, stood suddenly and spat into the flames.

'I'm not worried. It's the king's orders – no shame, no blame. My old man's a curse on my life anyway.'

'My mother says, she's had her life. Wouldn't want to be young now, she says. I'll wait till she's sleeping. Pillow her. She's weak anyway. Been giving me her share.'

As the second youth spoke, others began to wonder – how? How would each man dispose of his parents? They discussed the bravest way. Leaving the old to wander and fall over a cliff, or into a rushing torrent, was seen by some as cowardice …

'You must know what it is that you do.'

The night grew heavy and sick, the sky a strange colour like rotten fruit. They kicked damp leaves on to the flames, and the man who cursed his father stamped them out, as on his father's face.

The henwife's son had learned her potions. She sipped the

poison on her low, disordered bedding on the floor, her eyes on him all the while.

Up on the rotting thatch, a man barely past his prime was hooked and rushed sliding off his own roof. Arms wide as a gull's wings, he plummeted.

It was a long night; in the morning, pits were dug. In the evening, food was shared, still rationed, but enough. The man who had hated his father rebuked a younger one for his tears.

'They brought it on themselves. When they were young, they emptied the lake of fish. They cut down trees to build these homes and thereby changed the weather. They never cared.'

Through the long season, there was enough. The following year, crops grew; there was even a wedding. But the year after that, hunger returned, with mice that ate the grain, with mildew and frost, with mould, with flood. People looked at each other uneasily. Who was not worth saving now? Mothers held their babies close.

One man, a lean and quiet man, still spare and sometimes weak throughout the time of plenty, left the village one night, risking the curfew. None had noticed, but he had done this most days since the slaughter. Through the steep part of the wood, past ruins, between two massive oaks with roots that curled out and around, like sleeping serpents, with branches thick as trunks and trunks the size of a hovel, he strode, stumbled and slid.

Below the oaks was open ground full of leaf mounds, heavy with moss. Long ago, this could have been a working site, forgotten now, or a sacred meeting place; stones fallen where roots had pushed the boundaries of a built place, low walls still partly solid. The young man looked below, beyond the stream that marked a steep unwholesome boundary, to that trafficked highway of the woods. Few ventured further now.

Behind the fallen trunk of one great oak, beyond the stone walls, was a sudden cliff. In a strange fold of the rock was a cave, its mouth not as wide as a cry, nor open to consume, but a thin squeeze sideways, a doorway into darkness. It grazed his back, slipped him sideways in.

'Father.'

There was a movement in the spinning, strangely-coloured dark, and a throat cleared. The voice was almost warm-toned, almost strong:

'Son.'

The young man explained that he had brought only one crust and some berries. He told his father of the new disaster and the new fears.

'People are asking, who's next? Who can we kill? One of us even said we should … eat … the –'

His father grinned a bleak one-tooth grin, knowing for certain who that would be.

'Let me think. Sit there. Let me remember.'

So chill and numb his body, waiting, that the young man's body creaked when he stood.

'It gets too cold for you in here …'

'Plough the roads.'

'What? Do what?'

'Plough – the – roads. All. The old ones too, the abandoned ones.'

The young man asked no questions, but trusted his father's word. The damp air seeped into his shirt as he walked back home, leaving his leather cape behind, spread over his father's knees.

At the next meeting, he stood and said, 'Plough the roads'.

Packed earth roads that led from every home and ruined house, toward the mills beyond, were turned that week by men whose desperation stopped their questions. If any doubted, they were mute, or grumbled merely to their wives at night. Perhaps they thought that morning would bring mysterious changes; they stared at the deep scars of the impassable roads and suspected some plot. Nothing had happened. Worse, that night, and all of the next day, it rained. Trapped in their hovels, with the fretful sounds of hungry children or the terrible silence of their exhausted resignation, men sat hopeless. The man who had hated his father found that the repairs he had made to his roof were shifting, loosened by the water that puddled his mud floor. He had been sure to follow the old fool's instructions; he thought he had been sure.

None stirred from their homes for three days, and some chewed mildewed thatch to keep them from running mad. Talk had ceased, and the walls of each man's home were the limits of the universe.

On the fourth day, timid sunlight washed the morning. By noon, the air was dry, the mud stiffening. Still, defeated people lay in the humid hovels, suspicious, numb, awaiting death.

The next day was more golden, warmth penetrating the hovel walls, and some of the children were allowed to venture out. There was, in the minds of some parents, a plan to send the children to the king, to beg for a meagre share of the Royal larders. The King was fond of children, often saying they were the best of any civilisation, for they could change and bring change about.

A woman was sleeping, half aware, and her dreaming grew solid, insistent; she awoke with her daughter's voice close, her small hands tugging. When she sat up, still fuddled, the little one uncurled her hand, in which lay a bright green shoot.

Outside, villagers were gathered.

None spoke.

From the tower of his hall, the king looked on the valley and saw a young man, walking slowly, with a frail companion; not on the tracks, but straight across the barren fields. As they came closer, the king felt his anger rise, for here was walking a man who should be dead. He waited. Waiting, he let his eyes drift across the scene. Some new thing had happened, a pattern he had never seen, of narrow pathways glinting green joining each house and hamlet, dancing over every hill. As the walkers came close, he saw in their faces humble apprehension, courage; and, in the eyes of the ancient one, a look he was too young to understand.

Talespin

'No-one is listening. We're talking to ourselves –'

'Talking's not telling. Arguments on who's who and what's proper, you do realise there's less under your feet than when we set out? We need some strong stuff, something to make folk think, but … Mostly, a big effort. No showing off in between. Just … let them make of us what they will.'

Logan Sinclair

Perhaps I am unusual, perhaps not, in that an incident – an experience – of absolute immensity, one that shakes you and is a puzzle, if not an absolute horror, can sink so completely beneath the waters of life's mundanity; be a little catch, you might say, in life's rich tapestry, but one that leads to no unravelling, hardly noticeable. One would think it might tip all your perceptions upside down, and …

Well.

I had a frisson, I should admit, when the booking came in from Stannersley Old Hall. Didn't know why. Nevertheless, with everyone depending on me and our only just recovering from the last few awful years, I accepted the gig.

We pulled the company together, mostly young blood but one or two old friends. I never mind working with people in my circle who've always been there. We have mouldered along nicely together. It was a shock when Georgia Flynn breezed in. The last time I'd seen her she was striding about in red loon pants and a cheesecloth shirt, giving us a rather fey Viola. Not a bad actress, but the taint of training never left her. Perfect diction and a by-the-book interpretation, but nothing … you know. She was quite the sylph back then, with a rangy, 'gels'-school' manner. Now she looks like a dropped blancmange. Didn't cast her.

What I was saying about the effect of a strange … I must admit it took a few days for the mildew to lift from my spirits. Felt *distanced*, heavy, almost soiled, and the energy and colour all around me jarred; blinded and deafened me almost.

I'm getting ahead of myself.

We were going to play at Stannersley Hall. This was the first time round, you understand: a couple of standards, and something the family had unearthed that had been done, firstly for a wedding in the seventeen hundreds, then much later for another one, and it was quite a well-written piece. I was looking forward to recreating the magic, on the very spot ... you know.

Dean was driving, I was riding shotgun up in front, and the rest were gabbing ten to the dozen and singing in the back, and they all cheered as we swung into the entrance. It never gets old, and we only had the newbies with us. Ursula and Jim were driving up, as befits their station, in their beautifully converted field ambulance.

The evening sun flared intensely, blinding the windows, inflaming the red brick of a house whose appearance sickened me and shook me to the core. It was a pretty house, with tall ornate chimneys and gables; not as large as a Hall can be, with a row of garden centre pots either side the door crammed with red and blue flowers. The dread never left me as we were shown into the hall; stone flags and massive oaken chests contrasting with the department-store sofas and the electric fires in huge hearths. There were photographs on a Jacobean side table, one of a family group: the teenage boys affecting a casual pose; the mother, ankles crossed and neatly to one side, seated on a brocade couch; and the father, standing, hair curling on his collar, smiling ironically, it seemed to me, his thumb hooked into a thick leather belt, his pastel jacket pushed back and exposing a colourful shirt. A stone basin of toddlers in lacy garments from an earlier time; various horse or fancy-dress photos; it seemed to represent the legend, not the lives, of the family in this most photogenic of houses.

The Lady of the house, or her representative – remiss of me, but I had been rendered stupid and somehow deafened by the sight of the house when she made her welcome speech – bustled us up the stairs, showing first the two chambers reserved for the company, where thick foam beds had been lined up under the formidable menagerie on the chimneypiece in the men's quarters, and similar beds along the panelled wall opposite an intricately leaded window on the wide boards of the women's room. In each of the rooms a mound of new pillows and older quilts was slung on to the long tables. Incense burned, slightly masking the dusty odour.

Assurances were made that I was not condemned to the same camping arrangements, and I was spiralled up a narrow stair, the lady whisking out of sight at every turn, to a low and very worm-eaten door behind which was Mr Murgisson's flat. Mr Murgisson being absent, or possibly long dead, overnight employees of the hall and extra guests were quartered here, it seemed. Everything was coldly immaculate in terms of cleanliness and order. The furnishings were fifty years old and the bathroom was an appalling cell in sticking plaster pink and mud brown.

It was impossible for me to spend the night here. It made no sense. If I had believed there to be danger of any kind I would never have let Dean use the flat, which he was happy to do.

''Ome frum 'ome,' he announced with his long lopsided smile.

I clapped my hand to my forehead in a pantomime of regret.

'I am so sorry, my dear Lady, er ... How utterly thoughtless of me. After you had gone to such trouble, though I feel sure Dean will enjoy the privacy, yes, ah ... I have a friend here – near here – and promised to visit. Stay. He lost his wife only last year. I fear I must decline your ... Should have let you know. I will, yes, of course, no, that's ... I know the way, yes. Dean, give me the keys to the chicken crate. Yes, I know about the clutch. I will be careful. Nine o'clock tomorrow morning. I cannot apologise enough. This way? Thank you.'

If I had to, I thought as I jolted up the drive in the company vehicle, I would sleep on the back seat in some car park or other with a couple of cloaks over me; but as I drove into the next little town and looked up at a dramatic cliff that reared above the plain, decent Regency Crescent at its base, I saw what was clearly a hotel of the same vintage. There were lights in some windows, and the white walls were floodlit too. Almost immediately I found the way in, with a well-lit gate and a large signboard proclaiming this to be the New Heights Hotel. It was quite a steep and curving drive but there was plenty of parking.

Waiting at the reception desk to be allocated a room I turned to appreciate the setting. Through an archway there was a sparkle of chandeliers and a general sense of civilised, comfortable enjoyment. I could forgive the slightly worn opulence of the thick blue carpet and the overpainted plaster cornices with the melted ice cream effect because the place was so welcoming: the fragrance of good old cooked dinners, real dinners, with red wine gravy, roast parsnips, and bright green peas so familiar.

It had been a sunny day, but early in the season, and now the dark blue sky of evening brought with it a chill. I picked up a leaflet, hoping soon to be stretching out against smooth linen in one of the rooms featured; perhaps the red walled four-poster room, or the one with the modern king-sized divan and striped curtains.

The clerk looked up perkily and told me I was in luck: there were no rooms in the main house but there was one in the new annexe. I was both disappointed and grateful; doubtless the new wing would smell of paint and rubber-backed carpet, but at least it would be sterile, warm and convenient. I wondered how Dean was faring in the flat at the Hall.

I turned right, then left, as instructed, trundled along a corridor with gradually diminishing illumination, and found myself facing double swing doors with no further steps or turns. I looked back in case I had missed something, but there was only the way I had come; nothing at all to either side. The blinking, buzzing strip-light irritated me, but more so the trolley abandoned at an angle across the swing doors. I heaved it out of the way, and found the swing doors less accommodating than they might have been, too.

I found my room, but there seemed to be nowhere to use the key card. Fortunately, the door swung open at a touch.

The room was … brown.

Of course, any addition to a Georgian hotel would be termed the "new wing" for decades after its completion, but they could have made an effort; ditching the fake woodgrain wardrobe, for instance. The wallpaper, though also brown, was a fussy pictorial of birds and blossom in a faintly familiar style, and the headboard of the bed, beige quilted plastic, displayed a repulsive little hole picked out by one of the buttons, the perished foam poking through.

No good demanding an alternative room; this was the only

one available. One night, I told myself, and I would be on my way back to Deal, and sanity, after a rollicking performance.

The chill of that first sight of the Hall swept over me. I hoped it wasn't, then hoped it might be, an ordinary touch of fluey cold. It must be; it would account for the peculiar sourness I detected, and the sharp taste.

I slipped off my outerwear and slid into bed in my boxers and tee-shirt. And, I'm sorry, my socks. I was blessedly alone, after all. Thankfully, the bed seemed warm and dry. I was surprised, having predicted cold damp sheets.

I was thinking of my father. I could almost hear him: those crisp, light utterances, no palpable cruelty, but comparison, advice, and … If he began a critique he would stop himself, not wishing to waste his wisdom on someone destined to be a solicitor, or an antiques dealer, or even a hotel manager. Josephine, he mentored; Piers, he launched; once, I had missed a cadence and said that it made no difference to the text or the meaning; where did I find the nerve? He got my mother, I recall, and made her play the hypnotic trance scene from one of his blasted mystery things; only he told her to gaze into his ears. She was in hysterics, which of course was because of his elegant clowning; but I felt betrayed.

I left that house the next day. Ghastly Victorian fake.

I must have fallen asleep, remembering the walk up the drive, looking back at the sun flashing brass on to the windows and the vulgar line-up of red and blue sports cars. The crunch of my feet on the gravel sent me to sleep.

'Room service.'

'Room service, sir. Madam.'

'Oh, for goodness sake, Simon,' said a woman's voice, warm and with that little lift that gives an operatic tone to a speaking voice. Pure resonance, crystal drops of diction. There was the door, a man's voice, the squeak of trolley wheels, and then – I opened my eyes.

A flash of swirling purple and orange and a pinned-up pile of reddish curls. She turned. She wrinkled her nose and batted long, very blackened eyelashes.

I sat up. I looked down. I was wearing purple silk pyjamas, with short bottoms and a mandarin collar.

Who was Simon?

It seemed that I was.

I was attracted to my companion but did not like her. Somehow, and here, I don't know whether it was me or Simon, I knew she was – how can I put it? – planning, assessing, on camera as it were. What we might call, always "on". Like my father. Unlike my grandparents, to whose modest Georgian home I had fled. I say modest; it was substantial enough, with a sea view and thick, embracing walls. Barely any theatrical memorabilia and only a couple of fine antiques. Fireplaces, naturally; panelled doors, and a handrail like butter toffee soaring up the stairs.

I am not so hypocritical as to claim that my happiness at my grandparents' home was entirely due to their wise, kind treatment of me.

I like good things. I usually revel in the grand homes we play in. My flat in Deal, though boxy and boring internally, enjoys a preserved shell, and I have the cachet of the great front door and the wonderful windows. There's a fire surround too, rescued and fitted up as a cupboard. Internally sparse, the façade is gloriously authentic.

'You're very quiet,' says the woman.

Oh, just a moment – Heather. Her name is Heather.

'Adore my surprise, thanks. Your little bird is super happy.'

Waggling an orange box at me, she leans over and I am engulfed in Acqua– something. An overwhelming herbal, citrus fog clogs my throat. Her curl scratches my cheek.

I know her. She is my – Simon's – student. Or was. Intends to be – what? Who *is* Simon?

She sits on the bed, self-consciously eating prawn cocktail and licking Thousand Island dressing off her lips. One of us is captivated, the other repelled and cynical; but both Simon and I feel overwhelming, melancholy desire. I realise that the room is warmer, and though unchanged it appears to be smart, stylish and in good repair.

Heather leans forward, and I notice that the thick beige foundation fails to mask little pits in her cheeks. I shut my eyes, dreading the kiss, and hear her affected giggle as she pops a moustache of wet lettuce across my mouth. I cannot move.

My eyes won't open.

I am stiff and cold.

Am I dead, then?

If so, am I dead as Simon, or as myself?

Can I leave?

If I leave, where will I –?

There is a hand on mine. Someone takes a wet thing off my face.

'Sir, are you all right? Bit late to be out, getting chilly … Are you a guest, sir?'

I was on a bench in a shabby part of the hotel garden, and a man my own age was bending over me, a sycamore leaf in his hand.

The next few minutes were as disconnected as anything I

had ever experienced, but I offered no explanation, only apology, and the hotel staff decided between them that I'd decided to have a look around, straying out of the proper garden, and nodded off momentarily. They did ask about medical conditions, and I was accompanied to the New Annexe.

At first, I wanted to resist, until I was shown into the room. The approach was no dreary tunnel but a well-glazed atrium effect. My keycard worked and the room was warm. Pale walls, one large picture of a flowerhead with bee, and the best and hottest shower I have ever enjoyed. The bed so good it was almost wasted on me; I slept too soundly to luxuriate in it.

What else? Ah, yes: the prickle of unease I felt on approaching Stannersley Hall the next morning lifted like mist in sunshine. There was an odd moment when the Lady of the house enquired as to my friend's welfare, but I recalled my lie and blustered something. Another queasy moment when Briony appeared waving purple satin, but it was her practice skirt.

I asked Dean about his night.

'No probs, Captain. Course, I did 'ave a midnight visitor, but she didn't 'ave no 'ead, so I reckoned she couldn't see me anyway, so …'

'So you slept well. Good.'

'You all right, Captain? 'Ad breakfast, 'ave you? At your mate's?'

Dean gave me one of those looks.

'I will join the troupe and have a bite. Didn't have much.'

He gazed at me for a couple of beats and then turned smartly.

'Through 'ere. As it 'appens, I 'ad a very interesting time

with the old Lady's 'usband before I turned in. Likes vinyl. Got a lot of opera. Got some recitations an' all, your mum and dad doing that radio Shakespeare. You want to sign it for 'im, Captain. Put the value up. Watch your step. Now, if you got any sense, you'll tuck in. You look thinner than your own shadow. Ay ay, look who's come to sort you all out.'

As we entered the breakfast room it was like hearing a radio comedy, a favourite, whilst holding a funeral card. I knew them all, and I so wanted to be myself, be the Logan they all knew. But the benefits of the deep slumber I'd enjoyed receded like the tide. I almost heard its mournful whisper on the shingle. No one noticed, but they greeted me and returned to their anecdotes or arguments. I could tell the breakfast was good, though I tasted nothing.

Ursula sat beside me. Most underrated, complex actress I ever worked with. Subtle shades, no tricks. Wasted on my fadaddles, but she and Jim put in a summer appearance most years.

'Midway upon my life I found myself in a gloomy mood,' she said.

Her voice is like amber, with a thousand years of thought behind it. Yet she sounds utterly natural.

'Ursula, I am past the midway point. Thanks for noticing, but ... Work to do.'

'That's right,' she said.

A few more remarks and she went back to Jim, sitting close.

During rehearsal, a fleeting moment lifted my spirits. The action was on the main floor, but a couple of the girls were sitting in the window seat. I was moving around to set the sightlines and had a new idea, so I went and stood on about the third step of the stone staircase. Opposite, the two girls were pleating ruffs. More ruffs and partlets were heaped on the table beside them. The midmorning sun struck the window; the caps and collars gleamed and the girls were bathed in a halo of brilliance and crisp shadow. They resembled a Vermeer. There was no way I could achieve that with our rig.

I gave a few notes, made a change to some of the timing to stop one of the boys from stealing the laugh, that kind of thing. We tried a few alternative approaches to the denouement, which seemed muddled to me, though Ursula said everyone but me would know exactly what was going on. I didn't mind; she said it fondly.

There's an idea I'm mulling over: to have the cast come on in their own clothes and not acting at all. Just start to get ready … and as they put on the costume, they assume the character and diction. The transformation is like looking into a chrysalis at the butterfly assembling. It makes a strange enchantment, to watch and know yet believe otherwise; I see it in the faces of the audiences, those who linger to catch a word, dazed by the world we have created yet fascinated by us, our imagined lives, just as much as by the candlelight on brocade, and the proximity of a scene they cannot enter yet whose intensity is palpable, and lived. How wonderful, they say, to live such a life.

To the youngest they say, we'll look out for you on telly. To me: you look like Piers Sinclair, they say. Meaning no harm. A compliment. Some look, wry, shrewd, waiting benignly, but –

Should I tell them, do you think? Such a loss, Piers, a shooting star. My father never recovered.

No. I don't tell them who I am, or was, or what.

On with the motley, hey ring a ding ding.

Talespin

Across the fields there came ... not rain; perhaps an ambitious mist, a fine veil that kissed the skins of the Tales, but sent the page into a panic.

'Put me somewhere! Cover me up!' it rustled. 'I'm done for if I get wet!'

'You want putting under our cloaks to save you, now? Admit it, and then I will. You think you know it all, but you are our baby. Fine print and big ideas; but who shaped you? Come on, then.'

Pond

I used to destroy things I had made if they were praised by people I despised. Sometimes, even a gift from a loved one, because I feared its accidental loss, or even caring too much for it, I would burn or bury. Quite calm, yet not at peace, I would quell regretful feelings, which I perceived as self-indulgence.

Perhaps I should have been a nun.

When burying paper, I made a gift to the soil. Even gold was returned to the sleeping earth. Some prize only what has been wrought into goods of exchange, which display the maker's skill, the master's wealth. What nature yields they must transform or despise.

These acts occurred only rarely during my childhood and, later, in the days before my wedding. My mother never suspected; though if anything was missed, I was questioned with a gentle intensity that made me grieve for the gift but sealed my mouth.

One Spring I put my doll into our pond. I had seen the Girls' Day Festival dolls set out in their boat. I knew that in some ways my parents were modern people, attending such rituals only as a matter of tradition. They would never destroy my beautiful Hina to ensure my future success. Only my own diligence, and my father's generosity, could do that.

I was troubled, though; and so my precious Hina set sail in a banana leaf boat. A pond is not the sea. I had to throw stones to sink her. My parents' pond. I wonder what the new owners will think if ever they drain it?

This pond is thick like syrup. Drops fall, dead mayflies on the ripples bob like moored boats in the bay of Kagoshima.

Warm vapour rises from the earth, returning the gift of last night's rain to the heavens. Ferns growing around the water are lush, but where leaves drift they decompose.

Something buzzes endlessly.

I must decide.

Around the edges of the pond the water looks like whipped and bubbling matcha, and I imagine lifting the pond like a tea-bowl; I imagine its milky green and living skin bobbing against my lips. I imagine the feel of the pond water slipping down my throat.

There is no death, only a changed life.

I recall my grandmother. What is my duty to her? She is old. If I go to her, I might be able to nurse her, cheer her up, keep her well. If I go to her, the shame of my desertion might well kill her. She may summon my uncle to drag me back, and he will meet my husband, and my husband will be full of stern but gracious words, which will convince my uncle, and he will drive away and leave me with the man he does not know, and with his mother.

A frog sits on a moss-covered stone. I think he has been sitting, motionless, with a fixed eye, for a long time. When I notice him, he flicks out his tongue, whips a dancing, iridescent fly from the air and then flops into the water, which gulps him in beneath the algae, down among the stones.

Talespin

Until ...

The fire was burning low.

Tales were dispersed in pairs, wandering along the pasture edge, voices mingling as they flickered like shadows, sometimes merging. A few were more energetic, walking alone but aware of the others, breaking into a little dance, or standing, rapt and melancholy, gazing at the distance.

Ellafella sat by the embers, smiling wryly to himself at the pile of gathering ash. The farmer's Tale landed, light as a lilac feather, by his side.

'Where'd you get to, Love?'

'Here and there. I heard someone telling me, so I went to hear.'

'Tellin' you what? Oh, I get you. Well that's nice. You missed a cracker.'

'Oh, I heard it too. I was here as well as there. That's what I said – here and there.'

'I liked you, you came across very – truthful. Though you can't live on harp music –'

'Ah, but the daughter –'

'No need to explain yourself. Let folk see it, or come to it – or be told, if they want telling. No, you– It was grand, that. You're a lot braver than me, I tell you that. Going out just as you are, all misty.'

They sat. Other Tales joined them. There was some exchange of glances, shuffling to make space, but it was a while before any spoke.

The long silence got to the end of itself, so the Tales had to speak again.

'That was refreshing. I admire the printed page for its efforts of course, and we – the genesis of all communication – are the most useful and most stirring of all life-forms, but that silence was quite precious. Thank you for sharing it with us all.'

'A pleasure,' said the silence; then 'Ouch' as there was a sound like ice cracking.

A few Tales stood, most dwindling uselessly to appear concerned, but at a loss; Ellafella groped at the air.

'Got it,' he said, and made a sharp, compressing movement. 'Nay, don't talk, you'll break again. Stick to your own job – and yes, before you spoil it by asking, we have met. Several times. Especially in Norwich, in November, first house on a Thursday. Please, please, go to Stratford as much as you like, but please keep away from my kitchen scene.'

Silence departed, and everyone talked at once.

'It's all right to pause. We'll be worn out at this rate, and no one is listening.'

'Can we convene? Now, I think we understand that some of us have – mutated somewhat in our specific, ah, embrocations – no ...'

'Emanations?'

'As to how we're told, is that it? Well, say that then.'

'Thank you. The question is not whether it is right to ... confine us in books, or make us even into other art forms, no matter how populist indeed –'

'Ta very much.'

'Those of us of the greatest age, who do prefer a purist and more declamatory style in our delivery, must perhaps seek what it is that makes a Tale. Well, that's it, really.'

The ancient Tale paused and seemed to flicker. Others exchanged uneasy glances.

'Are we dying?'

'Not likely. Come on, as long as somebody, somewhere, is telling a story – one of us – a joke, even –'

'I must draw the line at jokes,' gasped the ancient Tale, sipping at a leaf of dew provided by Ellafella.

'Why? Because they're quick and silly? Don't they show truth? I'm in the way of being a sort of extended joke myself. There's a fool, and a comeuppance, and a punchline. I'm as old as you, and I come from the frozen mountains where the wild herds roam, and the village with no well. They tell me in the farms and in the inns after a song, and in city pubs with too much bad wine. I show folly, and upending, and punishment and glory. I'm in every language you can find, and many unwritten and dying. The thing about me is not that I am greater or finer, but that we are all mirrors, we are all dreams, we are the truth of all humanity. We cannot die until they do. As long as there is Truth in the world, and people, we will flourish. Leave the library. Shed your cobwebbed robes. The monsters, and the spirits, the dragons and the fools, the heroes and beasts – they are humanity, and we are not unlikely or fantastic. We are the fragrance of the commonplace.'

None were sure where the voice came from, but they all felt that they had spoken. It was an extraordinary sensation.

The Tales stood, taller than before. They had gained a glow of colour. Some embraced. They were ready to stride into the world, whatever they might find there, but expecting only welcome.

As they disappeared over the hill, Ellafella, his arm linked with an ancient Chinese Tale, who was strong and supple enough to support them both, said musingly:

'One thing I have noticed. People – you know, out there – when they're talking, and one of them doesn't believe summat another one just said – have you noticed this? – they say

"Oooh, what a Tale". I find that offensive. I might start a campaign.'

He fished for a handkerchief and blew his nose.

'Do you mind?' crackled the page.

Ellafella's teasing apology was lost on the wandering air as they walked over the green hill to far away. Caught in a dewdrop, the final Tale, left behind but unafraid, awoke and considered itself.

The Potter and Lady Truth

Nothing had changed since he was happy.

Nothing had altered since he was content.

His wife annoyed him no more, delighted him no less, than formerly.

The mountains, in dawn light or midnight deep, looked as far and near as ever, watching him climb or come home to the one room with the one lamp and the mat spread upon the floor.

His wife asked him what was wrong, and he said, nothing.

The second time she asked, he said he did not know.

The third time, he said he needed to know.

She asked him what did he need to know, and they almost smiled when he almost joked, that … he didn't know.

One morning, she said to him, go and find out. I'll wait.

He knew that if he did not go, he would still be restless; yet his wife's being so selfless made him want to stay with her. She said he must go now, and he had one year to find the answer.

He walked backwards, waving, until he could no longer see her, and he put his foot wrong and fell as he turned …

He walked the world over. No one abused him, but they could not tell him where he could find the truth. At least, he knew now what he was seeking.

One day, in highlands very like those of his home, he stood in a straggly pasture looking up at the distant peaks. A man with sheep came whistling by, and his dog crouched by him as he halted, beating the grass with its tail. The shepherd said the dog was friendly and had taken to the stranger. The man asked; and to his incredulous delight, the shepherd knew where Truth could be found. Most people didn't bother her much, he said. She was way, way up there, in a cave in the mountain.

Invigorated, the seeker scrambled, climbed, sweated, slipped and wobbled his way up a far higher slope than those of his home. He stood at last at the open mouth of a great cave.

At his back was the world he knew, though he was far from home. The darkening air cooled his back, and the road home beckoned; but what good would it do to turn back now?

He could see nothing ahead of him, not even whether there was a cavern floor, a plunge into black waters, or a well deep as the world that would swallow him up. He closed his eyes and thrust out his foot.

There was a smooth enough path between the rocks against which he sometimes stumbled, and as he went onwards it seemed that the darkness clenched itself into shapes, or dissipated into grey. So he managed, until, at the end of the cave, he faced a shape that was no rock; it was a living being.

'You have come far, and you are welcome,' he heard, in the sweetest, warmest, most musical voice he had ever heard.

He swallowed before asking, a little fearfully, his own voice like a straw blowing across a stone floor: 'Are you the Lady, Truth? I have come to learn from you.'

He waited as she turned to face him. He knew without thinking that Truth must be as old as Time. But nothing could have prepared him for the shock, the terror, the unwilling but absolute repugnance that shook him and almost sent him tumbling, scrambling, out of the cave and down the mountain.

She held out her hand, though, and the wonderful voice soothed him, and her words inspired him, and he sat at her feet and listened. For a year he listened, and learnt and understood such things that none but he could tell you – unless you go and find her for yourself.

After that year, she told him he could return to the world and to his kiln, his wheel, his mountain and his wife. He thought of his home with joy, and some concern, so gathered his bag and put on his hat with great eagerness. But at the mouth of the cave, he turned.

'Forgive me, Lady,' he said. 'In my speed I have forgotten myself. You, who have taught me so much – is there nothing I can do for you? What can I say, what can I tell them?'

He could no longer see her, as she merged with the shadows of the dripping cave; but her voice, quiet and calm, wrapped him like the fragrance of a rose at sunset.

'Tell them I'm beautiful.'

About the Author

Growing up in Wharfedale, a step from Brontë country, and later in Derbyshire where she still lives, Gillian was fortunate to be commissioned to write and direct an immersive promenade production of Jane Eyre in Haddon Hall, where so many versions have been filmed. She also provided the chilling sounds of Bertha Rochester from various hidden locations around the Hall.

In 2010 she joined Matlock Storytelling Café and developed an interest in oral telling as an art distinct from acting, and discovered a wealth of stories and folklore.

If you have enjoyed this book, please consider leaving a review for Gillian to let her know what you thought of her work.

You can find out more about Gillian Shimwell on her author page on the Fantastic Books Store. While you're there, why not browse our other delightful tales and wonderfully woven prose?

www.fantasticbooksstore.com

Printed in Great Britain
by Amazon